IMMACULATE CONCEPTION

– A NOVEL –

I.J. MILLER

IMMACULATE CONCEPTION

Island Publishing
New Jersey, USA

Cover design by Willsin Rowe

ALSO BY I.J. MILLER

SEESAW (novel)

WHIPPED (novel)

SEX AND LOVE (short story collection)

CLIMBING THE STAIRS (novella)

WUTHERING NIGHTS (novel)

For my beloved Kathryn. Your kindness, patience, and love inspire me every day.

PART ONE

MOTEL

"I'm less unhappy when I sleep," mutters Al, so tired she's barely able to form words as she collapses face first onto the motel bed.

Maddie, lying on the other bed, is tempted to say, *you never sleep*, but Al's already passed out. Probably better this way. Any inkling of a challenge would lead to another one-sided argument that Maddie would surely lose. She is exhausted as well. She closes her eyes. She wishes *she* could sleep. But her pulse continues to race at highway speed, knowing that after a few hours rest they will finally be able to complete their cross-country trek and be safe amid the millions living in New York City.

From the east, the Hudson County Sheriff, followed by his deputy, in matching cars of blue and white, pull into the lone driveway of the motel parking lot. There are plenty of empty spaces, making it easier to avoid the giant potholes puddled from the rain. Only one guest vehicle, a muddy Honda CR-V with New Mexico plates, is in the lot, parked in front of number fifteen, the only room occupied at this early morning hour on a cold Tuesday in March.

The forty rooms horseshoe around this stretch of asphalt marked by faded lines. At the end of the lot is a lobby with a picture window. Behind the glass is a small neon sign, one missing the letter V, that flashes repeatedly the word *ACANCY*.

From the west, a New Jersey State Trooper arrives. All of the vehicles congregate in a cluster at the center of the parking lot. Each man behind the wheel is quite familiar with this motel near the last chance exit off 495, a final alternative before driving into the darkness of the Lincoln Tunnel and emerging into Manhattan. It's a place that typically rents by the hour: drug dealers, pimps, prostitutes, and johns, *guests* who feel Weehawken, New Jersey is safer and less expensive.

Their orders are simply to wait for Nokenge, who's driving the seventy-five miles from the state capital, accompanied by his personal four man SWAT team.

Their only concern is the two women behind the door to room fifteen.

And the baby.

AL

Alice loved Sunday mornings best. Her daddy always made her pancakes before church.

And now that she was seven, he let her help.

He cracked the eggs into a metal bowl, added milk and pancake mix. Alice focused hard, and without spilling a drop, stirred and stirred, performing magic just for him, as she made the lumpy yellow and white liquid transform into a smooth cream-colored batter.

"My little wizard," he declared.

She beamed.

"Which would you rather have?" asked her daddy, "a magic wand or a magic carpet?"

"Both," answered Alice. "I'd fly around the world performing magic for children who don't have daddies or mommies to make them breakfast. I would feed them *en-chanted* pancakes!"

"A noble cause."

He knew that after church she would set up her stuffed animals and dolls as poor people, then magically appear from behind her pillows, use the bathroom mat to *fly* off her bed, while she waved her umbrella *wand* and conjured up an abundance of pancakes for all. He was glad that, as a motherless, only child, Alice kept herself happy with the joyous and plentiful imaginary games she played in her room.

When they were done eating, she helped clean up, then went upstairs to brush her teeth and dress for church. This was when Daddy usually turned into Mr. Bear.

Alice heard him growl outside her room. She let out a pretend scream. He flung open the door, still in his jammies, and she shrieked, "Oh, no, Mr. Bear, you're back!"

"Still hungry!" snarled Mr. Bear, as he chased her around the bed and she laughed and giggled and threw stuffed animals at him.

Chest hair overflowed through his V-neck white tee shirt and curled into a big black ball. Thick strands cascaded down his chubby arms. He hadn't yet shaved the dark scruffiness along his face. He had a big bear belly, wild bear hair, and big bear paws that finally caught her and scooped her up as she squealed, "Mr. Bear, you're so strong!"

"Makes it easier to swallow you whole!" he growled.

He threw her on the bed and tickled and rough-housed her, while Alice pretended to struggle, until tears of laughter streamed down her cheeks and she screamed, "I love you so much, you great big powerful Mr. Bear!"

Inspired even more, he cuddled her closer, gobbled her belly, and made hungry bear sounds. Then he held her so tight she almost lost her breath, his furry face buried deep in her long black hair.

There was a final quick shudder that ran through his body as he pressed against her, then a sudden calm, then he released her.

"My sweet Alice," he whispered, nearly out of breath.

Mr. Bear gone, Daddy back, he stood and glanced sadly towards the night stand at the smiling photo of Alice's mother, his deceased wife. He said, "Time to go to church and pray."

He added something that always bewildered her with its impossibility, "Daddy loves you too much."

MADDIE

It was not easy for Madeline, a child of nine, to make her mother's bed, especially because Mother was still in it: lethargic, but awake, unwilling to take her meds.

She used the sheet to push Mother to the other side. Mother hated to be touched, especially by a *germatoid,* as Mother would say, like Madeline. After one side was made, the top sheet and blanket neatly tucked in, the pillow fluffed up, Madeline got Mother to roll back but stay on top of the blanket while she finished the job.

"All neat and cozy," said Madeline.

Mother smiled warmly. That was her, just like a halfway made bed: one side neat and proper, the other side a mess.

Madeline took advantage of the smile by offering the glass of water on the night stand, the round blue pill (the one to relax Mother and make her feel good), and the small white pill (the one to control Mother's facial twitching caused by the blue pill).

Making the bed had worked. Not only did Mother take the pills without a fuss, but she said, "Tomorrow's Christmas, isn't it? Let's go shopping."

Mother took special care to fix her hair and apply makeup before they began the one mile trek to the stores. Madeline let their dog Barky down the back fire escape of their apartment to fend for himself since they were out of dog food, then found the food stamps to restock the fridge.

Once outside, Mother undid the umbrella and held it over their heads.

"Rain makes me sad," said Mother.

Madeline thought of asking why then did they end up in Oregon, but she knew better.

They stopped at the department store first, one packed with shoppers. They wandered the aisles, looked at fluffy bathroom towels, TV sets with remote controls, puzzles, games. The more they shopped the more Madeline became her age, buzzed from the bright colors, the newness of everything, the intensity of parents snatching stuff off the shelves and filling their carts. Madeline ran ahead. She directed Mother to a display of portable phones. She pointed to a cool dog bed for Barky. The *mature* Madeline warned herself to tone it down. She knew they didn't have money to buy anything.

But Mother had already stopped walking as fast. She began reacting to things with a deep sigh, or a loud *hmph*. If her smile this morning had been a beautiful northwest rainbow, her expression now leaned towards a stormy downpour.

"Let's go home," blurted Madeline, stopping short of grabbing Mother by the arm.

"Do you need another daughter?" Mother asked a young housewife dragging two little ones by the hands. The woman pretended not to hear.

Mother approached a teenage cashier, already frazzled from the long line of customers waiting impatiently at her station.

"I would like to leave my daughter here," said Mother. "She likes it so much, she should stay."

The cashier gave Mother a dirty look, snapped her gum, kept punching the register.

"Mother, please!" implored Madeline.

"I demand to speak to the manager!"

"Lady," said a chubby man, holding his credit card, balancing a kid's bike, "the loony bin's at the back of the store."

The customers laughed.

Tears streamed down Madeline's face as Mother went down the line, making eye contact with each of the seven patrons waiting their turn to pay.

"I'm fully prepared to wash my hands of this *not beautiful* little girl."

That was when Madeline took off running, telling herself that she didn't care whether Mother made it home or not.

She didn't stop running until she made it to the apartment, where she headed straight to the twin bed in her tiny room next to the bathroom and buried herself under the covers, the *loony bin* line, the pitying stares, *not beautiful* making it difficult to breathe through her tears.

It was much later, pitch black, when Madeline heard Barky's wail, loud, deep, in pain, followed by the thwack of hard slaps coming from Mother's bedroom. Madeline was afraid of what she might see, but she knew she must protect the dog. She edged down the hall. There was a lamp on in Mother's bedroom and Madeline peeked in, but did not see Barky. Mother had hiked up her nightie, and, with an open palm, repeatedly and harshly, slapped her own inner thighs and wailed like a dog.

Madeline streaked back to her bed and smothered the pillow over her ears. There was nothing she could do. Mother would not take meds in this state of mind.

A few hours before dawn, Madeline quietly tiptoed back to Mother's room. The lamp was still on. She could hear Mother's deep breathing. Madeline shut the light, gently pushed Mother to the other side of the bed. Madeline slipped under the covers, inched towards Mother, their bodies spooning as one, as Madeline replicated the zig-zag of Mother's bent waist and knees. She breathed in deeply, taking in the familiar scent of Mother's hair, so much stronger at this proximity. The only upside to one of these spells was Mother's deep exhaustion that followed. It allowed Madeline to pull herself as close as possible, flesh to flesh, the joy of this loving embrace making this day better than most.

MOTEL

Maddie hears the loud slam of multiple car doors. She opens her eyes. She did not sleep. She walks to the window, pulls back the curtain. She sees the state trooper car, the two sheriff cars, a white Ford sedan, and an unmarked black van. She sees all of the law enforcement personnel head towards the Ford. Maddie lets the curtain slip from her fingers. She turns, sees Al still deep asleep. She runs to the bathroom, drops to her knees, then lets out long deep sobs as tears drizzle down her face.

Nokenge labors to exit the Ford, working his heavy legs to the side, sliding his large belly out from under the steering wheel, lifting his 240 pound frame up from the seat. He is only five foot six, which makes him the roundest police officer in the state of New Jersey. There is only one job a police officer his size can hold: hostage negotiator.

The driver of the unmarked SWAT truck stays put, and so do the four hand-picked SWAT guys inside, rifles ready, bullet-proof vests strapped on.

Nokenge makes sure everyone else is in front of him when he speaks.

"Forget all the shit you've read in the papers, seen on TV about these two."

The group nods mechanically.

"All I'm concerned about is their *true* history, what we learn today, and what these two women intend to do."

Nokenge focuses on the deputy sheriff, a tall, lanky man with a protruding Adam's apple, who stares aimlessly over Nokenge's shoulder at the cars whizzing by.

"Am I boring you, Gomer?"

The others snicker.

The deputy goes eyes front.

Nokenge's glare turns immediately towards room fifteen.

"Fuckin' Thelma and Louise with a baby! Total…tabloid…bullshit! Have they killed anyone?"

"They hurt someone," says the state trooper.

"That's what I'm fuckin' talking about! Only *one* of them hurt someone. You have to understand them as two distinct individuals. One stabbed, the other didn't. Is it because one's more dangerous, or she just happened to have the knife? Comprehend these things and we'll grant the governor his number one wish and fulfill my current life's goal: no baby gets hurt on my watch!"

He looks them all in the eye, assessing who can actually be of use. The deputy completely wilts under Nokenge's stare, this bowling ball of a man boring right through him. He lowers his head, stammers, "I, uh, thought Harvey Keitel's character did a great job in *Thelma and Louise*."

"They drove off a fuckin' cliff, numbnuts!" snaps Nokenge. He turns to the sheriff, a man in his fifties, face shading red with embarrassment. "Make sure this guy does nothing more than coffee."

Maddie dries her face. Before waking Al, before telling her that the worst has arrived and their journey is over, she walks to the motel room's dresser. The bottom drawer is pulled out and baby Jesse is asleep, swaddled in his blanket. She picks him up, holds him close, strokes his dark hair and tells him how beautiful he is. She prepares a bottle and holds it to his mouth. Jesse begins a greedy sucking.

This is her happiest time in life, feeling this deep connection, nurturing Jesse, feeding him, giving him life, helping him grow.

She can't help looking over at Al, tossing now, still asleep, but mumbling in a deeply troubled tone.

Maddie doesn't know which is worse: what's out there, or that she will soon have to wake Al and tell her what's out there.

"Everyone needs to stash his car around the side of the building," continues Nokenge. "We're not blocking off the access road because that's a red flag. First weather chopper flies over and every tabloid in the country will swarm this area. First suspicious motorist with a camera phone and we're all over YouTube. I'll position the SWAT guys and the driver will get rid of the van. I've kept this off the air and it's crucial you do the same. Don't tell a soul, not your wives, girlfriends, not even a text, where you are, what you're doing, or I'll have your badges." He looks at the sheriff and the deputy. "The only reason you two are still around is that I personally need to make sure you both keep this under wraps." To the sheriff, "Take Barney here and stay in the office and make sure the desk clerk doesn't budge, doesn't check anyone in." To everyone: "It's essential, if we want to be successful today, that we keep this thing from becoming even more of a media circus."

Jesse finishes his feeding and Maddie gently pats his back until he burps, then she swaddles him again and places him in the open dresser drawer. She sits on her bed and stares at Al, still reclined, eyes closed, on the other side of this small, dingy room.

Madeline notices that Al's very short hair, parted in the middle, is barely out of place, despite her extended lack of sleep and restless nap. In high school it was a mullet. Now it has a short, square back.

Maddie's own hair had always been a blondish brown, but in the last few years, in her mid-twenties, it turned a ghostly white. She has had the same Dutch Boy style since she was five years old, like the kid on the paint can, always cut by her mother, complete with straight bangs framing her plain face.

They both wear the same khaki pants, loose and baggy, and identical, oversized, short sleeve polo shirts, only Al's is black and Maddie's is white. Though they look nothing alike, they have the same round looseness of body. The baggy clothes mark no lines on their frames, no contours of breasts, no definition of waist.

Maddie wills herself to stand and approach Al's bed, her legs as heavy as steel beams. She drops to one knee. She knows better than to touch Al. She shakes the bed.

Al's eyes flicker open. It takes another moment for Al to become fully conscious, to realize she is in this seedy New Jersey motel and that Maddie is staring down at her.

Al knows Maddie's expressions well enough to understand instantly that they've hit the end of their road.

"I should've kept driving," says Al. "We were so close. It's my fault. I'm so tired." Her eyes flutter closed again. "I wish I could sleep more."

Sometimes Al's calm scares Maddie more than her ire.

Maddie retreats to her bed.

Al forces her eyes open, gathers energy, stands, walks to the window, lifts back the curtain, then turns to Maddie.

"I don't see anything."

"There were four police cars out there earlier and a black van. They're probably hiding now, waiting to make their move. We've run out of options."

"No we haven't!" barks Al, a sudden surge of red flooding her face, voice so loud that Maddie flinches and Jesse lets out a sharp cry.

The young trooper approaches Nokenge inside the motel office. He's six foot four, blond buzz cut, cheeks shaved a smooth pink, not a wrinkle in his traditional light blue uniform blazer. "Sir, I had the floor plans to the motel sent to my PDA." He hands the plans to Nokenge. "Behind the rooms is a crawl space then a solid stone wall. Room fifteen adjoins fourteen. Would you like me to requisition the plans for the heating and cooling ducts?"

"The old vent system surprise," says Nokenge. "Why didn't I think of that? Works in every hostage movie ever made. Like they wouldn't suspect that. Like I can find a trained midget cop who is small enough to crawl through motel ducts. Like the noise wouldn't thunder directly to their room before he got there." He hands back the papers. "I already have these."

"Yes, sir." The young man turns to leave.

"Trooper," says Nokenge. The officer turns back. In a voice that helps this rookie understand even more clearly the depth of Nokenge's focus on the task at hand, in a tone so serious it communicates a level of respect for the trooper's efforts, Nokenge says quietly, "There will be no storming rooms here. No sneak attacks, no unexpected visits, no coming through the windows or the roof. And, as God is my witness, no shooting. If we can help it. I have one job and one job only." He stares the young trooper head-on, eliciting a silent nod. "*Talk* them into giving up the baby."

AL

The organ music rose to the ceiling of this small stone church and eight year old Alice felt her spirits soar with it.

She was on her knees, in the row with others from her Sunday school class, the girls all in white, the boys in dark suits, as they awaited their first communion.

Her dad stood in the back of this crowded church, praying fervently. Alice knew how proud he was. At the house, when she had shown off her dress with a quick twirl, he had told her how beautiful she was and that he had looked forward to this day for a long time.

Alice let the music, the prayers, the priest's melodic voice wash over her. She truly felt the spirit, reveling in her pure state of grace. Some of the boys giggled. A few girls handed out candy. Alice thought back to her first confession last weekend, the final test to make sure she understood right from wrong. She had expressed remorse for using the word *shit* twice, for being envious of her best friend's beautiful mother, for not putting away her dolls and stuffed animals like her dad had requested. The priest had assigned her seven Hail Mary's and told her to go in peace and that she was forgiven.

And now, just as it was time to rise and march down the aisle to the alter, she recited: "Lord, I am not worthy to receive you but only say the word and my soul shall be healed."

When it was her turn to kneel, the priest looked down upon her with the kindest of expressions as he said, "The body of Christ," and placed a wafer on her tongue. She took a sip of wine from the chalice. The flooding sensations from the tastes, the music, the prayers made her head swim and she never felt so happy. Giant Jesus on the cross hanging on the wall in front of her never seemed so real.

Later that day, her dad threw a party in her honor at his favorite Scranton watering hole. Only his buddies attended. Alice's lone relative on her mother's side was an aunt who lived in Texas. Her dad never talked about his family, somewhere down south, especially Grandpa.

They toasted her all afternoon, played music on the jukebox. Her dad's friend offered her a sip of beer, but she wanted nothing to taint this beautiful moment, to wash away the taste of the holy wine. Still in her white communion dress, she danced with her dad as she stood on his feet and he floated her around the room, completing her perfect day.

"I love you so much, sweetheart," he said.

"I love you so much too, Daddy."

It was nighttime when Alice tenderly held his hand and helped him up the front porch and into their house. He had had way too much to drink, which, lately, was not uncommon. There were less pancake breakfasts, but there was still Mr. Bear.

At the top of the stairs he began his growl. She jumped away from him and scurried to her room. "Oh, no, it's Mr. Bear!" She slammed the door behind her. His growl increased outside her door as she mock-yelled for help. He burst into the room and she flung a stuffed dinosaur at him.

"All dressed up to be my special meal."

He chased her a bit, but soon became dizzy and sat on the bed.

"You okay, Daddy?" asked Alice, suddenly full of concern.

He let out a roar and flung her to the bed.

"You tricked me, Mr. Bear! You mean giant ball of fur!"

As usual, he rough-housed her, tickled her, gobbled at her stomach, his mouth at her white communion dress as he pulled away layers of lace.

"You really are beautiful," he said in a puff of sour alcohol breath, confusing her again because he used his Daddy voice.

But then he was back to Mr. Bear, baring his big bear teeth, his big bear paws squeezing all over her body as she giggled and laughed and pretended, with playful glee, that she wanted him to stop.

At these moments she never felt so loved by him. He held her close, his face, once again, buried deep in her hair.

But then he did something unusual.

He grabbed her right hand and pulled it to the muscle by his leg. Alice knew he had that heavy muscle. She had felt it against her, sometimes seeming to move by itself. But it never felt this big. It scared her and she tried to jerk her hand away.

"You look so grown up in your dress," Daddy whispered. Then he hiked it up and nibbled at her stomach. This did not seem like Mr. Bear and she struggled to pull her dress down because he could see her underpants. Instead he held both her wrists together in one meaty paw. It had to be Mr. Bear. It didn't look anything like Daddy. It looked like a *mean* Mr. Bear: eyes bloodshot and wild, gelled hair sticking out like stalks of fur. Then she suddenly breathed backwards, rapidly, swallowing her breath in gulps. And the light went out—not in her room, but in her brain—when Mr. Bear's angry claw touched her. She remained frozen, unable to let on how much it scared her. And then she had to cry out. He stopped, but did not leave. He stood over her, as tall as the priest when she had kneeled in front of him. He took out the muscle by his leg and with a few shakes, and a quick gasp, wet her communion dress, then left the room.

She was still too frightened to emit even a peep. No tears flowed down her face, yet, on the inside, she felt an anguished wailing. She finally understood what her dad meant when he said he loved her too much. And though she would never set foot in a church again, she finally understood completely the overwhelming power of her communion:

She was not worthy and indeed she was old enough to know right from wrong.

MADDIE

"It's time for you to start wearing makeup," said Mother as she brushed Madeline's Dutch Boy cut into perfect straightness.

At fourteen, Madeline had been selected to be the assistant manager to the JV basketball team, and the captain, Lu-Ann, had invited her to a team party, which surprised Maddie because she had assumed, by the way the team randomly tossed dirty towels in her direction, that she was invisible to all of them.

Mother had bought Madeline a new dress at the Goodwill. Madeline wasn't sure about the dress, but the last party she had been to—a fifth grade birthday party—all the girls wore dresses.

The problem was Madeline's acne: red blotches, whiteheads, blackheads sprinkled all over her face like an Everything Pizza. Before bedtime, Madeline usually scratched sores, severed scabs, popped pus-filled pimples until there were rows of milky dots on the mirror's surface and trails of blood running down her face like tears

Mother usually implored her not to pick and squeeze, explaining that it could lead to lifelong scars.

At the vanity, Mother educated while working on Madeline's face, explaining base, cover-up, blush, mascara, lipstick and eye shadow, careful to avoid skin to skin contact. Madeline was thrilled with this opportunity to be fussed over.

When Mother was done, Madeline thought she looked a little too *colorful*, but nevertheless was amazed by the transformation. All of her acne had disappeared, and with her hair combed, decked out in a dress, she felt like a new person.

Madeline had dreamt for so long that when she began high school things would be different.

Lu-Ann answered the door at her house and immediately seemed shocked by Madeline's *new look*. She escorted Madeline to her finished basement, where ten basketball girls and six boys were munching on snacks, talking, listening to music.

Madeline was about to turn and sprint home. Everyone wore jeans and casual tops. The makeup on the girls was teenage light, while Madeline was middle-aged beauty parlor. Lu-Ann put a comforting hand on her shoulder and said, "It's okay."

Madeline retreated to a folding chair in the corner. She willed herself to become invisible, like at school, walking down the halls, practically melding with the lockers, completely unnoticed, as if she was an adolescent specter. She wanted to stay, wanted to watch and learn how teenagers socialized: a few girls danced with each other, the boys huddled on the other side of the room and occasionally broke into loud guffaws.

Then Lu-Ann flicked the lights on and off and told everyone to sit in a circle on the floor. Madeline tried to make herself as small as possible, but Lu-Ann motioned for Madeline to join the circle, which she did.

Nobody snickered or commented. Maybe she really was invisible?

Lu-Ann explained the rules for Seven Minutes in Heaven. If a girl spun the coke bottle and it landed on a boy you *had* to go into the closet together. If it landed on another girl, it was a do-over.

"Unless you're both *lezzies*," added Lu-Ann, which drew a hearty round of laughter.

Madeline's body trembled with anticipation. She had never kissed a boy. She had wanted to for so long. Girls spun, got paired off, went into the closet with a boy, and came out beaming with huge sheepish grins. Then it was Madeline's turn. She heard a few snickers, but she didn't care. It would finally happen.

And the bottle landed on Alex, a pitcher on the JV baseball team, dark hair and eyes, part Spanish. Lu-Ann swooned with jealousy. Everyone knew she had a major crush on Alex.

A perfect gentleman, he stood, bowed, helped her to her feet with a delicate grasp of her hand, guided her towards the closet, and said, "Ladies first."

She started to step in, but actually was pushed, just as the door slammed behind her and the bolt slid on the outside lock.

"Not if she was the last bitch on the planet!" Alex told the others. Their laughter pummeled its way through the slats of the wood door and swirled around her, echoing like cannons. The tears flowed easily, streaking her makeup-laden eyes and cheeks.

She heard the chant of "Dork, dork, dork!" the loudest voice that of Lu-Ann's, the party reaching its liveliest height. Madeline understood now why she had been invited.

It was a long Seven Minutes in Hell, but when the door finally opened, Madeline raced up the stairs— droplets of shame whipping off her face as if she were a cartoon character—and didn't stop until she made it home, the *dork* chant painfully squeezing her eardrums.

Before entering her apartment, she tried desperately to stifle the crying and wipe her eyes and face on the sleeves of her dress. She prayed that Mother was already asleep.

But she wasn't, having stayed up to get a full report.

No matter how hard Madeline tried, the tears continued to flow as they sat on the couch. No matter how much she wanted to make up a story, like the party was great and she just fell on the way home, she couldn't help filling Mother in on all of the gory details. Madeline hoped desperately for some comforting words, some explanation as to why kids were so mean, or Madeline so off.

But the more Madeline talked, the more uncomfortable Mother became. She got all twitchy in the face and started making sounds instead of commenting.

Just as Madeline was sure Mother was about to cap off the worst night ever with a typical harsh comment, she saw Mother take the deepest of breaths, close her eyes tight, seemingly will herself to stay calm and not show disappointment in her only child.

For this small kindness, Madeline was about to break the house rules and reach out to hug Mother and tell her how much she loved her, how having a mother made life easier.

But Mother stood, and to Madeline's surprise, slowly unbuttoned her blouse.

"It's all for the best," said Mother, with true sincerity. Mother pulled aside the nylon material and, for the very first time, displayed the full angriness of two, large, purple scars stapled down Mother's chest where her cancerous breasts had been. "This is what boys see when they look at you."

MOTEL

Inside room fifteen, Al begins to eat. Not really eat, binge. On sugar.

She starts with powdered donuts, then slabs from an oversized chocolate bar, washing everything down with 100% pure grape juice, all of the stuff that fueled their marathon trip cross country.

Maddie immediately snatches Jesse from the dresser drawer, holds him tight, whispers endearments, intent on protecting him from the brewing storm.

"We never should've stopped here," fumes Al, her mouth full. "They would never find us in a city as big as New York." She swigs more juice. "If only you were a better fuckin' driver!"

Maddie fights off tears.

"How the hell did they find us in this dump?"

"We're all over the news," says Maddie. "Somebody must have recognized us."

"Did I ask you?" barks Al.

It's no use, thinks Maddie.

"We need a plan," continues Al, pacing, eating, mumbling. "We've gone too far, accomplished too much to rollover in this armpit of America...second only to Scranton, PA. They gotta know we mean business!"

Perhaps it's the sugar shocking Al's pancreas, or her basic athleticism, but with one manic blink of an eye, Al snatches Jesse from Maddie's grasp, has the blade out from her Swiss army knife, and exits through the door as Maddie screams, "No!"

With the baby completely swaddled, only the dark head sticking up, his cries developing into a deep howl, Al uses her left arm to hold him against her body, careful not to touch the baby's face with her bare arm. She doesn't see anyone, but knows there might be snipers on the roof, so she keeps her back against the motel door.

"Come on out, motherfuckers!" she screams.

Nokenge, the sheriff and the deputy are in the front office, **NO ACANCY** now flashing in the window. All three scramble outside.

They are forty yards away, but Al shouts loud enough so they hear her clearly. Instinctively, she understands that Nokenge, in his oversized blue suit, white shirt, and red tie, is the boss, and she stares directly at him.

"I'm no Michael Jackson playing Baby on the Balcony, you sonofabitch!" She waves the knife with her right hand. "I will do the deed if you come anywhere near us! You want a Waco in Weehawken?"

Al ducks back into the room, passes Jesse off to Maddie, face crimson with emotion as she flings the knife, point first, into the wall. Maddie immediately retreats to the other side of the room, soothes the baby. Al drops heavily onto the bed, another round of pure exhaustion crashing in after the intense sugar rush.

"Sorry," she says. "Just trying to protect our family. I know I'm an asshole."

Al punches herself in the face.

Maddie cries out in pain; Al remains impassive.

In the parking lot, the sheriff and deputy stare at Nokenge, who for the first time is speechless, without the cocky jut of his jaw, his dark complexion gone ashen.

He goes back inside.

The deputy looks at his boss quizzically.

The sheriff whispers, "He was at Waco."

AL

As soon as Alice opened her eyes the morning after her communion, the pain flooded her body and mind. She stuffed her soiled white dress into a plastic bag, then carted it out back with the rest of the trash.

"Good morning, sweetheart," her dad said at breakfast, as if nothing had changed.

Everything had.

No more pancake breakfasts and Mr. Bear.

Nothing girlie so her dad would think her less beautiful.

Bad grades. Frequent fights. No friends.

Just her dad drinking and terrorizing her at night.

Perhaps his biggest sin was the stealing of her imagination. What had been rich and playful, became dull and dark, like her bedroom closet where her dolls, stuffed animals, and rosary now lay permanently cloistered.

Each night he came to her room, she tried to make herself more blank, more malleable, more of a non-person, believing that someone who cast no shadow would hurt less than a real human.

She had urges to pray, deeply, to ask God to make this end, but she no longer believed in a merciful God, one who forgave those who repented. She had done all he asked and at the moment of her greatest purity, she had been made impure.

She threw herself into the sport of softball, the out-of-town tournaments providing bonus nights away from her dad. The fundamentals, the familiar thwack of the ball off her bat, the mechanical feel of doing something over and over that required very little imagination provided some escape.

Her hips grew wide, her body stocky and strong. She smoked pot regularly, developed a need for sweets, the sugar fueling her ability to practice long hours.

At fifteen, she became the star third baseman for Scranton's top travel team and grew a ridiculously long mullet. She had no interest in boys or girls, though everyone thought she was a lesbian. So repulsed by flesh to flesh contact, she was the only girl who walked the line at the end of the games and refused to shake hands.

She took the field in the bottom of the sixth inning versus a team from Altoona, Scranton up 5-1. She had already hit a home run and a run scoring double. In the visiting bleachers was a boy, long oily hair parted in the middle, scraggy moustache, black leather strap on his left wrist, who thought he was one bad motherfucker. He was clearly the boyfriend of the opposing pitcher, a perky blond girl who redid her ponytail out of the back of her hat before every inning while flashing him a flirty smile.

Al was used to the usual visiting fan banter: "which team do you really play on?" and had no problem tuning it out. But he waited for when everyone was quiet, then screamed through the fence, "Hey, Inbred! Is it true that after your parents divorced they were no longer brother and sister?"

Several Altoona fans laughed heartily.

At the end of the inning, she told coach she needed to use the bathroom, which was a brick building on the other side of the parking lot where they were constructing a new storage shed. She spotted a thin, one inch nail, scurried back to the lot, and found Bad Boy's car, one she had seen him go to for more smokes, a black Camaro with cheesy orange flames painted across the hood. With a hefty rock, she drove the nail into his rear tire, just enough to create a slow leak.

At the dugout, she was able to sneak a scissors out of the trainer's med kit and into her own bat bag.

Back onto the field, three quick outs, and the game was over. Al saw Bad Boy give his girlfriend a kiss just before she boarded the bus. Then he finished his cigarette, got into the Camaro, and left.

Al only had a learner's permit, but she already had a car, a secondhand Honda CRV her dad had bought her so he didn't have to drive her around anymore.

Instead of going home, she headed towards the one lane road that accessed Interstate 81. Just a few miles down, she saw the Camaro parked on the side, Bad Boy jacking it up and about to change his flat. There wasn't much along this stretch except undeveloped lots thick with trees and bushes, an occasional house, and one tavern. She pulled over behind the Camaro, got out of her Honda.

Bad Boy looked at her, a bit confused.

"I don't need any help, dyko!"

He obviously didn't read the full menace in her face, nor notice the scissors in her right hand, nor the heavy rock in her left. But he felt the blow.

He was much taller and though she aimed for his chin, she got his chest with the rock, but it was still effective enough to knock him back into the deep grass, crack his sternum, and have him gasping for air. She was on his chest immediately, the scissors at his throat as he wheezed with extreme pain. If he knew how close she was to sliding the scissors forward into his throat, he might have screamed for mercy.

She cut off his hair, leaving him a bald splotchy mess. He was smart not to say a word, just trembled under her with large bug eyes. She told him that now his head matched his bogus moustache. She told him he needed to watch who he opened his mouth to with his sicko comments. She added, for a final bit of drama, that if she ever saw him again, she would kill him.

Al had gotten away with a lot during her years from eight to fifteen: the fights, the attitude, at worst leading to a couple of school suspensions or dismissals from teams. Perhaps because she was a softball star, perhaps because she was pitied because of her mother's early death, authority figures were usually flexible.

Not this time.

Al stood defiantly before the judge. Bad Boy was there with his parents, his hair sprouting like an unevenly planted garden. He refused to look in her direction. He would've seen her smile. Her dad had already contributed his usual, "no mother" line.

"Despite your outstanding softball career," said the judge, "your checkered history of poor grades, truancy, and after-school fights leaves with me very little wiggle room for sentencing. Do you have anything to say on your behalf?"

Al turned towards her dad, who sat behind her. He took a deep breath, held it, his cheeks puffing out.

She was strongly tempted to expose her father not as the hardworking, single dad raising a daughter he had presented himself as, but as the horrible rapist he had become. One who used his penis as a weapon of destruction. She wouldn't do it in the hope of getting a lighter sentence. She would do it so her dad could understand a little of what her nightmare was like.

She heard her dad's big sigh of relief when she shook her head no.

It was simply too horrible for anyone to know.

"Six months in Juvenile Hall," said the judge, who banged his gavel and left.

She exited the court room in shackles, without even a nod towards her old man. She was exchanging one hell for another, but even Juvie had to be a lesser hell than home.

She did learn one valuable lesson.

The world is made up of two kinds of people, the *caught* and the *uncaught*. She was surely now one of the *caught*, foolishly doing nothing to conceal her identity during her quest for revenge.

Her dad was one of the *uncaught*.

She vowed never to be *caught* again.

She vowed to change his obscene status as well.

MADDIE

Madeline and her best friend Anthony walked down Main St. on a Saturday night.

Fellow teenagers cruised up and down this long strip, the boys and girls checking each other out, changing cars, hooking up. Not much had changed in McCannville, Oregon in the last forty years.

Anthony had a clear complexion, nice sandy brown hair, and perfect teeth. He was the first person she had shared Mother's psychiatric history with and recently had revealed that Mother had been in a state institution for the last month. In return, he had told her his father loathed him and was kicking him out of the house in a few months, right after graduation. Why? Because he was gay. Not openly, he had never *come out*, but everyone knew. McCannville was not a great place to be a homosexual.

To their misfortune, just as they made it to the center of town, Little Stu cruised by in his daddy's pick up, heading the opposite way, alone. Alone because he weighed 300 pounds, had extreme garlic breath, and not one nice bone in his body. He hooted his horn, gave them the finger, blasted them with the very unoriginal, "What's up, faggots?"

They didn't even look his way.

But Little Stu did a quick U-turn, parked in front of them, and lumbered his way back on foot.

"You guys too gay to hear?"

No college for Little Stu, just a life sentence milking cows on the farm.

"Madeline's not gay," said Anthony.

"Then why's she with you?"

Little Stu doubled over so extremely with laughter he could almost see his shoes.

They tried to move on, but he grabbed Anthony by the collar. "Where you going, homo?" He dragged him towards an alley.

"You're hurting me," said Anthony.

"That's the least of it," said Little Stu.

"Stop!" shouted Madeline as she followed after them. Little Stu took a wild backhand swing. Luckily his arm was too fat to move quickly. Madeline ducked and he swiped pure air. Anthony looked at Madeline, his eyes warning her to stay away.

Little Stu yanked Anthony behind the hardware store. She heard cursing, grunting, slaps, and yelling. Get help? Call the cops? She knew Anthony would not want the attention. He never reported it when his father smacked him around. Madeline toyed with the idea of grabbing one of the metal trash can lids and letting Little Stu have it. She berated herself for being such a coward, just like she was when Mother acted up in public. Too damn embarrassed.

She finally got up the nerve to walk to the end of the alley. Before she got there Little Stu made the turn towards her. He faked a slap and she cowered. He grinned and kept walking.

Anthony sat on the ground, head buried between his knees. She helped him up. He looked away. His face did not seem bruised, though his cheeks were red and his eyes moist.

At her apartment, next to each other on the couch, she asked, "Do you need ice?"

"He didn't really hit me."

"What did he do?"

Anthony stuck his index finger inside his mouth, mimed a blowjob, then began to sob.

"Oh my God!" cried Madeline.

She instinctively grabbed Anthony and pulled her to him. He cried in her lap and she stroked his hair. She told him he could stay with her tonight and anytime. She would always be his friend. She would take care of him. He said he would like that. He put his arms around her waist and she warmed to the feel of him squeezing back.

"You're so right when you said a lot of guys are gay in this town," said Madeline. "We should report him to the sheriff. I'm a witness. He can't be allowed to get away with it. He might do it again."

The two friends looked at each other.

"You really don't understand, do you?"

"What?" asked Madeline.

"He's not gay. He only picks on me because no girl would have him and he's too cheap to pay a whore. And this isn't the first time."

"All the more reason to call the sheriff."

"My dear Madeline." Anthony reached towards her face, oblivious to her acne, and stroked her cheeks without an ounce of inhibition. "He doesn't force me to do it. He's definitely rough, but he would stop if I really insisted."

And then it was like looking into a mirror, their expressions so helpless. It was like shit happens, you don't know why it happens, you can't help it from happening, but know it happens because you're the ultimate lonely loser.

They hugged each other tight.

She made popcorn and they watched TV into the night. She gave Anthony Mother's bed. She caressed his head one more time and was pleased that he sighed happily when she kissed his cheek. Just before falling asleep in her own bed, Madeline had one more ultimate lonely loser thought:

Little Stu, a straight guy, had chosen Anthony over her.

MOTEL

The phone rings in room fifteen. Startled, Jesse lets out a loud cry from the dresser drawer. Al picks up the receiver, says, "Go fuck yourself!" Then hangs up.

The phone rings again. Al picks up and Nokenge starts to speak, but Al says, "Didn't I tell you to go fuck yourself?" then slams the phone down again.

Maddie has already scrambled to the dresser for Jesse. She paces the room, bounces as she walks, tries to stop his crying. Still subdued after her sugar crash, Al takes a moment to notice how beautiful they both look together: Maddie staring at the baby with big blue eyes full of love, Jesse staring back as he is reminded, once again, how *safe* he is with his family.

So fucking close to having the life we dreamed of, thinks Al. *Only to get fucked at the last minute.*

Nokenge hits *one* and *talk* again on the cell phone he had programmed to speed dial room fifteen. It just rings. He hangs up. Knowing about her stint in Juvie, her pre-disposition towards violent, erratic behavior, having just witnessed it himself in front of their room, he is pretty sure that Alice is the one answering the phone, and the one who just unplugged it.

"The sandwiches are stale," says Maddie.

"Better than prison food."

Al lies flat on her bed, puts the pillow over her eyes.

"They're not going to let us set up house and stay here indefinitely," continues Maddie.

"I know."

If it was during her sugar binge and the subsequent rush, Maddie wouldn't be saying a word, but she takes advantage of this calm period.

"I'm worried they'll just storm the room and Jesse could get hurt."

"That's why I let them know I'm a crazy motherfucker."

"We should at least talk to them."

"My name is Nokenge," they hear through a bullhorn, from the parking lot.

"It's *fatfuck*," murmurs Al from the bed.

"There's nothing more I want right now than to speak with you," he continues.

Maddie puts Jesse back in the bottom drawer. He gurgles sweetly and waves his hand at her.

Maddie pulls back the window shade. Snow has begun to flurry, but Nokenge is only in pants, jacket, shirt, and tie. The bullhorn is in one hand, a pizza box and small plastic bag in the other. "I am the one who can help you. I can talk to you all day from here if you want."

Maddie plugs the phone jack back in. Al glares, but lies still.

"It's cold out," says Maddie. "He's just going to bellow with that thing and it's embarrassing."

Nokenge places the bullhorn on the ground, speed dials again, is pleased when he hears, "hello."

"Thank you," he says into the cell phone. "Is this Madeline or Alice I'm speaking with?"

"It's not relevant at this time."

He's sure it's Madeline. From the profiles he has received, his intuition tells him that she might be the key. Yet he is also wary about someone who let it go this far.

"I'm very serious about helping you and I have the full backing of the governor of the state. You must understand, considering your circumstances, that help from someone you can trust is extremely important."

"Is the pizza still warm?"

"Yes. And I also have some baby formula, pre-made so you don't have to use any water from this dump."

"You must be a daddy."

"I am," lies Nokenge.

"Can you promise no funny business?" asks Maddie.

"No wire, no weapons, no electronic device in the pizza. Just me."

"Bring it."

She hangs up.

Al jerks up in the bed.

Maddie says, "I'm hungry."

There is a soft knock at the door. Maddie opens it, but stands close to the doorway. She takes the pizza, places it on top of the desk. Nokenge deliberately holds onto the plastic bag with the baby formula. Over Madeline's shoulder he sees Alice sitting on the bed, knife in hand, the baby next to her.

"I'm sure you both understand the full meaning of the word *advocate*," says Nokenge. "That's what the governor has assigned me to be. I'm charged with the responsibility of bringing all three of you back to Oregon and assisting anyway I can." Just to the right, on top of the dresser, he notices a wallet, car keys, and prescription pill bottle. "Give me a chance to help you."

Al stands. "How about giving us a chance to close the door?"

"May I come in?"

"I don't think that would be best for your health," she responds.

Maddie extends her hand. "Are you going to give us the formula?"

He slides over the pill bottle, takes notice of the label *Seroquel*, places the bag on the dresser space he cleared.

"Now I really need to close this door," she continues. "Too drafty for the baby."

Nokenge blurts, "It's only a matter of time before the media sniffs this out and the whole situation at this motel goes as viral as your cross-country trip, which wouldn't be good for anyone, especially Jesse."

They are surprised to hear him say the baby's name.

Maddie looks at her partner.

Al shakes her head no.

Maddie is about to close the door.

Nokenge says, "Please believe me, Madeline, the fact that you're the biological mother will go a long way."

AL

Juvenile Hall reinforced two important concepts for Al, who immediately got punched in the face by her muscle-bound cellmate, Jo, when Al refused to shake her hand:

1. Be a tough sonofabitch.
2. Don't take shit from anyone.

Al explained that the handshake refusal wasn't because Jo was black, but because Al didn't like being touched because she had an asshole father who raped her. Jo understood and they became friends.

Jo was feared by everyone, which meant Al was feared by everyone, which was good, because Al wanted to keep her record as clean as possible to get out as soon as possible. Even the guards were nicer to them.

It was a miserable six months, being taught at a fourth grade level, watching her back all the time, piss-awful food, and no softball. But mostly she hated being locked up, being controlled by others. It was like being at home.

But Jo had a way of getting things through this one guard she knew, using a currency Al was not willing to spend.

Jo got Al a glove and softball that allowed her to practice throwing and fielding for hours off the yard's brick wall.

Al had developed a vaginal infection before arriving, but refused to go to the infirmary. Jo got her some cream. It didn't cure it, just made the itching and scratching more tolerable.

When Al's time was up, she hoped to take the bus home, but she was still a minor and needed to be released to a guardian, which was, of course, her dad. He was smart enough not to say anything, nor offer to help her with her small suitcase when she approached his car, perhaps taking notice of her physique toughened in the Juvie weight room, her cold-hearted, eyes-front death stare (now perfected) that was essential for keeping all unwanted bodies away from her.

He dropped her off at the house then went out to drink.

It was late, she was in bed, but hadn't slept a wink, her body wired from head to toe as she waited for him to come home. Her vaginal infection was worse than ever and she scratched and rubbed so vigorously, desperate for any kind of relief, that she bled.

Finally, he trudged up the stairs. In her hand, under the covers, was a kitchen knife. Any fear she felt at Juvie was a cakewalk compared to the tremble that volted her body as each step got closer. She knew all of his sounds: the steps to the bathroom, the ones to his bedroom, and the most dreaded of all, loud and thunderous, the ones that brought him to her room.

She heard him pee, then bump his head and curse, then retreat to his bedroom. She heard his body hit the mattress, followed soon by his loud, animal snores. She inched the knife up from under her covers and placed it under her pillow, and finally let out what seemed like her first breath since his car had pulled up.

She was not sure exactly what she would do if he came to her. There was no way it could be guaranteed she could get away with stabbing him, no matter how detailed she was about her life with *Daddy*, and sharing the shame was still one of the last things she wanted.

But mostly she feared returning to the world of the *caught* again. Jo had warned her, recounting tales of her own mom, that Juvie was Disneyland compared to the State Pen.

But she couldn't let him rape her again.

If it was pre-Juvie he might've gotten the jump on her, since she had dozed off. But in any type of prison, the hearing becomes acute. The snoring stopped. She reached for the knife, kept her hand outside the blanket this time. Then steps to her room. The door opened. Her breath came out in heaves. Beads of sweat popped from every pore. Now by the bed, standing over her, his beer breath, always nauseating, smacked her in the face.

"My sweet baby girl."

He was on top of her, but before he could mutter another word, the knife was at his throat, already drawing blood. The moon was bright enough so she could see his eyes bulge with surprise, could see his wild hair, his ugly unshaven face. He kept perfectly still. It could be all over with one deep plunge. She could do it this time. Maybe Bad Boy didn't deserve to die, but her father certainly did.

Some survival instinct froze her hand. She told him that this was over, that if he ever came near her again she would kill him, that there was no way he could ever fall asleep again without wondering if she would kill him during the night.

He looked at her tenderly, smiled, and said, "My darling, Alice, how I've missed you."

With one swift motion, echoing her own athleticism, he jerked her wrist away from his throat, twisted her arm so hard the knife dropped to the floor and her shoulder wrenched from its socket. She saw the rage and lust in his eyes and instantly peed the bed in anticipation of the beating of a lifetime.

But what he did was worse.

He turned her over, held her face down, which didn't take much effort since she lay as limp as a rag doll, and penetrated where he never had before.

The next morning, she waited until he went to work. She showered, only able to use one arm, the ache in her shoulder nothing compared to the pain in her rectum, the pain in her rectum nothing compared to the torture in her soul. Even after six months in Juvie-hell he was still the only person in the world she was afraid of. He showed her she wasn't as tough as she thought, and that she would take shit from him every time.

A man as ugly and vile as he, owned her.

She packed some bare essentials in a knapsack, stole the $223 dollars from the cookie jar, found her last stash of weed under the mattress. She left the heavy wood front door wide open as she hobbled down the porch steps for the very last time. She was relieved the Honda turned over, expertly peeling out of the driveway with one hand, as she gunned the car towards the highway.

There was relief that she was leaving everything behind, but no joy. No joy because somewhere back there, locked deep in a musty closet, was her childhood. She refused to look back. She knew much ended for her at the age of eight, and that what happened should not happen to anyone, especially a child.

She drove west, then south. Even with just one good arm, it took her only three days to make it all the way to her aunt's house in Texas, fueled by donuts, candy—wrappers everywhere that she tore open with her teeth—and marijuana. She never had to tell her aunt what her father had done. The blankness in Al's eyes, and surely the way her arm hung limp, told her aunt that Al's presence must be kept a secret, and the child, still only fifteen, needed an abundance of tender loving care.

Her aunt offered to drive her to the hospital. Al said she first had to make a phone call.

Al dialed the number of the Scranton police, a number she had brought along. She gave them her dad's name and address, but refused to give her name. She told them that if they went into the back room on the first floor there would be a large wooden desk. In the bottom drawer on the left side, under some papers, they would find a manila envelope full of explicit photos of men having sex with children. She added that considering the large quantity, there was definitely intent to distribute.

Al hung up. She would write Jo and thank her for smuggling in the photos before Al was released. She wished she could've been there when the police raided her father's home, if only to welcome him to the world of the *caught*.

MADDIE

It was late spring when Mother returned home from the hospital, a month before high school graduation. Madeline escorted her on the bus. When Mother had been admitted, her hair was colored a brownish blond, but now all of her gray had returned. The flesh around her eyes were crinkled into complex crow's feet. Madeline could see deep furrows along Mother's lips. But despite the aging, there was something that was more serene. Mother glanced casually at the beautiful Oregon flatlands through the bus window, head never turning sharply, rather her focus seemed to float calmly from one view to another.

Afraid to speak until they were completely away from the hospital and on the bus, Mother confessed that the state institution was a living nightmare and Madeline must promise that Mother would never be brought back. Madeline said she would do her best.

Haldol, that was the new drug the psychiatrist had prescribed. "An anti-psychotic showing wonderful results everywhere," he had told her, as if she were the parent.

And now, as the bus motored home, Mother hooked her arm through Madeline's and let out a smile as sweet as candy.

At the apartment, Mother was quick to notice how clean everything was, done in honor of her arrival. Madeline would like Mother to meet Anthony, but they were no longer friends. He got into a group who liked to sniff anything, from glue to paint to gasoline, and had stopped going to class, and was in danger of not completing senior year, perhaps his own twisted way of thwarting his father's threat to kick him out of the house after graduation.

Each morning, Mother made her own bed. They shopped together using food stamps, holding hands all the way to the supermarket. The old beauty parlor welcomed her back and with extensive coloring, fresh makeup, and a new haircut, Mother took years off her appearance. It was a week of pure bliss.

Madeline wanted to wait longer to discuss college with Mother, but deadlines were approaching. At the dinner table, as both finished eating the scrambled eggs that Mother had prepared, Madeline said, "I'm quite pleased to tell you that with a combination of academic scholarship and financial aid, all of my costs will be covered at Oregon State. I can come home anytime, including most weekends. I think it will be fun to experience someplace else aside from McCannville."

Madeline thought it best not to add that Oregon State was also a place so large that no one, well just a few from her hometown, would know what a loser she was.

"I want to study pre-med. I want to be a doctor."

Madeline studied Mother's face, looking for any twitch or shake. She listened for inner grumblings. But all was still, all was quiet. Until, "That's wonderful, Madeline. I think you would make a splendid doctor."

Wouldn't it be great to be the kind of doctor who discovered something like Haldol.

They cleaned up together. Mother offered to do the dishes. She said that at the hospital, believe it or not, her job had been kitchen duty and she had been told that her work ethic was impeccable.

The next morning, after Madeline popped out of the shower and was about to get ready for school, she noticed Mother in the living room, wearing a nice mid-length skirt, ironing a blouse. What surprised Madeline was that Mother was wearing a bra stuffed with something flesh-colored and rubbery. Mother smiled and said, "They gave it to me at the hospital. Said it would improve my self-esteem."

"Sexy," declared Madeline, all smiles.

She turned to go back to her room, when Mother asked, "And is a germatoid like you sexy?"

Mother's tone sounded pleasant, but the use of *germatoid* spread a caution through Madeline's chest. She turned back. Mother unplugged the iron.

"Did you find a boyfriend while I was gone? Where's this Anthony you told me about?"

Mother lifted the iron with her right hand.

Madeline was speechless.

"Has he fucked you yet? Of course not. You have boobies, but you still have the acne."

Mother stepped closer, the bottom of the still-scalding iron facing forward, a few feet from Madeline's face. Madeline retreated a terrified half-step.

"What are you afraid of?" Mother asked, her words a bit slurred from the Haldol. Without even a wince, she pressed the tip of the hot iron against the inside of her forearm. "Not so bad."

"Mother!" shouted Madeline and Mother immediately lifted the iron, her skin already red and blistery, flesh coming off her arm in a ropey strand.

Madeline grabbed the iron's handle and gently took it from her hand.

"Don't touch me!" snapped Mother.

Madeline ran cool water over the damaged skin. She applied antiseptic cream and bandaged the arm, doing her best not to have flesh to flesh contact. There would be no emergency room, because that would mean an explanation, a report, and a possible return to the state institution.

The next day, Madeline sent her enrollment documents to Lancer College, the local school. They didn't have a formal pre-med program, but had decent health sciences. With the financial aid she received there, Lancer would also be for free.

As long as she lived at home.

MOTEL

"Thank you," says Nokenge, after Maddie finally allows him to enter the motel room.

"Certainly not my choice," says Al as she glares at Maddie.

Maddie closes the door. Nokenge pulls out the wood desk chair, flips it backward near the door, between the two beds, and lowers his heavy frame. He rests his thick arms on top of the chair's straight back.

"It's not important whether you like me or not," says Nokenge.

"We don't," says Al.

"But you know as well as I do that sooner or later something's gotta give. Which makes me your best friend."

"Good," says Al. "Then get us a plane with enough gas to fly us to Samoa. They have no extradition treaty. Throw in a couple of hundred thousand as well."

"I can tell you I can do that, but it's highly unlikely it would happen. And between here and boarding a plane, there are about fifty different ways to—"

"Then what the fuck use are you?" barks Al as she bolts up in the bed.

Nokenge remains perfectly still. "The most important thing that has to happen today—and I'm sure you'll agree—is that *everyone* gets through this safely."

"Let him finish," says Maddie.

Al sits back on the bed, face etched with agitation.

"Thank you, Madeline," says Nokenge.

"I prefer Maddie." She looks towards the other bed. "Al."

Al looks towards Nokenge. "Asshole."

Nokenge focuses on Maddie.

"Let's take a really close look at the current situation. There's no escape route and this rat trap is no place for a baby." Maddie nods. "You'll face a custody hearing in Oregon. As I said before, as the biological mother much is in your favor."

"Can we keep him while all of this is going on?" asks Al, sharply.

Nokenge takes a deep breath. All of his answers are of monumental importance. He's not adverse to lying, but also needs their trust.

"Considering everything that has gone down, I can't promise it."

Al looks at Maddie. "Let's kick his ass to the curb." Al gives Nokenge's ample frame a full once over, then shakes her head. "No, he's going to have to cart his own fat ass out of here. Now!"

Al is on her feet again. The knife is in her hand. The baby begins to fuss. Maddie immediately goes to Jesse, picks him up, which distracts Al. Maddie looks at his perfect tiny features, the dark eyes, the long black lashes. She couldn't bear losing him. Her heart is so full of love for his beautiful, kind face and so full of sadness that it has come to this.

She says to Nokenge, "Tell us the truth, please. What are the chances we both will be granted custody? Especially after Chicago."

Nokenge had anticipated this question. "The governor of New Jersey has already reached out to the governor of Illinois to discuss leniency."

Maddie catches Al's eye, trying to communicate how positive this news is. Al sits back on the bed.

Nokenge follows up with, "But the longer this goes on, the more laws you break, the harder it's going to be to get what you both want. So let's end this now. Walk out with me. I'll take you to the airport. The baby will be safe."

Maddie says, "We want this child to have a good life, the life we can give him, the life neither of us had."

"I believe it's possible."

"You lying piece of shit!" says Al, leaping back to her feet, steps from his chair.

Nokenge knows he's in danger. He knows why her father did prison time and would lay long odds that she was abused as a child. But he can't let her dominate the situation, which is why he doesn't stand, raise a hand, twitch a muscle, but is also completely ready to defend himself.

"You know damn well that if we surrender I go to jail!" continues Al as she paces furiously. Jesse begins to cry, loudly. "And the baby goes to you know who."

Nokenge pulls his arms off the back rest, shifts in the chair, ready to stand if he needs to.

"And even if that doesn't happen right away," adds Al, "and we post my bail, we won't be able to see Jesse, take care of Jesse while the judicial system takes its time sorting this shit out. Even if we had a chance for custody we would probably rot somewhere waiting while some fucked up temporary foster father, just for the fun of it," Al stops pacing, moves closer to Nokenge, "would put his hands on—"

"Wait!" says Maddie, her abrupt tone halting Al, who is now inches from Nokenge, gripping the knife even tighter. Maddie steps between them, says, "I think it best you leave now."

"I'm only trying to—"

Maddie slaps him across his face.

Everyone is shocked. Nokenge manages to stay calm. He rises slowly from the chair. He says politely, "Let me know if I can get you anything else."

He exits the room.

Back in the motel lobby, Nokenge's concerned expression does not go unnoticed, and the sheriff immediately asks how it went.

Nokenge says, "Forget Thelma and Louise. We have Patty Hearst with a baby, following the lead of a one-woman, bi-polar, Symbionese Liberation Army."

AL

At the age of seventeen, Al accepted a full athletic scholarship to Southwest Tech, about an hour outside of Laredo.

One week into the fall season, during practice, Al took out the catcher and team captain, Crystal, on a hard slide home. Five foot eight, 160 solid pounds, all-girl brute, Crystal took exception, not liking this cocky freshman from the get go. Al offered to settle it after practice.

Coaches gone, players forming a circle, the two went at it. Clearly Crystal had her own demons, because she fought with an intensity Al had not seen, even at Juvie. Al got knocked down, she got back up. A tooth was jarred loose, Al spit it out. Her right eye swelled, one was enough. Most of the team, except the freshmen, cheered Crystal on, but as the fight wore on everyone got quiet and uncomfortable from watching a beating that was thoroughly ugly. Crystal eventually wanted to stop, but this punk freshman wouldn't stay down. Finally, with blood gushing out of a nose that was clearly broken, Al remained on one knee.

"Welcome to college," said Crystal, extending a hand.

Al refused it. Stood. Knocked Crystal cold with one punch.

A week later, as she left her dorm, Al was jumped and immediately covered with a burlap sack. She struggled, but there were too many of them. She was thrown into the trunk of a car. She heard the boys laughing as they drove away. She heard other cars following. She heard multiple bottles crash on the asphalt as they drove. Someone shouted, "Alpha Beta Pi rules!"

The cars eventually stopped and she was led inside an abandoned barn, cursing, trying to head butt anyone she could, though it was difficult because she was completely blind under the burlap sack.

They tied her hands and ankles. She was placed on her knees. The sack was removed.

It was pitch black, but she knew they were out there.

"You're all going to die!" she shouted.

A spotlight was turned on, blinding her, though she could tell she was surrounded by a dozen college boys, clearly this year's pledge class, all naked, except for Halloween masks.

"Guns up!" shouted a voice from somewhere in the dark. The frat boys grabbed their dicks and began to stroke.

Cautiously, they inched forward, as close as twelve people can get around one person on her knees, close enough so she became nauseous by their stench of alcohol as they continued to stroke with vigor.

There was a moment of silence from Al, as she tried desperately to hold it all in, gritting her teeth, refusing to reveal her pain, doing all she could to make this initiation less satisfying for the pledges.

But she couldn't last.

From her mouth came a scream that could only be likened to a wounded animal, not just an animal that was shot or bit, but one caught in a giant steel trap that was slowly severing a limb. Only for Al, the sight of drunk men jerking off and about to come on her was just another amputation of her soul.

"Stop!" one of them suddenly ordered, the one wearing an Arnold Schwarzenegger mask.

The voice from the dark barked, "Pledge, know your place. Fuck up now and you will be dismissed!"

The pledge bent down, tried to comfort Al, but she shook him off. He stood up, said to the group, "Get the fuck out of here. Everyone! Or I will personally kick the shit out of each and every one of you." His tone was deadly serious and the frat boys retreated. Soon Al heard raucous laughter and gravel crunching as cars peeled away.

Al looked at the freshman standing over her. From his naked body, she knew he was an athlete, clearly defined six pack, near-perfect muscular frame marred only by the distinct protrusion of a bulging left rib. He took off his mask and threw it away. She recognized Wynn Davis, the number one freshman basketball recruit.

Perhaps he was being kind. Perhaps he knew someone had to stop her sick howling. Perhaps he knew he could get into any other frat he chose because he was Wynn Davis.

He untied her, draped the burlap sack over her shoulders to stop the shivering.

Either way, Al was grateful.

Wynn found his clothes, dressed, escorted her to his car.

On the way back, she asked, "The president of Alpha Beta Pi is Crystal the softball captain's boyfriend, isn't he?"

"I believe so."

She saw Wynn a couple of times on campus after that, usually with a hot girl on his arm, and was prepared to ignore him completely, but he always smiled and said *hi*. One evening he was leaving the fitness center the same time she was. He asked, "Do you party?"

She almost answered, "I sure do," though she didn't party as much because pot was getting more expensive and she didn't have her dad to steal from anymore, but instead studied his face, trying to ascertain his intent. She followed him to the rear of the library.

They shared the first blunt, back and forth, then lit up another, as they stared at the hundreds of stars in the clear Texas sky. They both welcomed the soothing peace it brought their brains and bodies.

Al studied Wynn again, the dark hair, the perfect handsome face that must have gotten him laid, easily, since his early teens. She liked that he didn't ask why she had screeched that night like a stuck pig.

"You wouldn't ever try to fuck me, would you?" she asked, sure she knew the answer, but compelled to ask anyway. Any guy who had ever been nice to her, sooner or later, put on a move.

Wynn said, with a boyish grin, "Not if you were the last girl on earth."

Al laughed. Then Wynn laughed.

Al said, "I think you and I are going to get along just fine."

MADDIE

Lancer College was simply a left turn off the state road, a 200 acre campus, most of it the football field and adjacent bleachers. The one dorm housed the football players. Most of the 900 other students commuted, which meant about half of Madeline's high school attended Lancer and knew she was a dweeb.

During freshman orientation, Madeline decided to go by Maddie, a more grown up name.

Boys didn't want to date a Maddie either.

Her advisor confirmed that it would be difficult to get into medical school from Lancer, but encouraged her to become an athletic trainer, as there were many high school and college jobs available.

Her senior mentor suggested a local singles phone chat line would improve her social life.

That was how Maddie became Destiny.

Why not be blond and tall, with perky breasts and a perfectly smooth, cream-colored complexion?

On the chat line, she was often complimented on her sexy voice. She worked on her Destiny speech: slow, sultry, almost British. She discovered that men liked when you called them *baby*.

Destiny had a loving mother and father who traveled a lot, a weakness for skiing Mt. Hood, dabbled in modeling, but was serious about her studies. She could tell that some didn't believe her, but she doubted that all the boys looked like their descriptions. How could so many muscled college jocks with great cars be on this line?

Devin soon became her favorite.

They talked late into the night, after Mother went to bed, on the one kitchen phone. He liked her breathy whisper (which was more about not waking Mother). He was respectful and didn't talk dirty, but shared that he was lonely, recovering from a bad break up, and finally ready, after so many date downers, to meet a girl who wasn't superficial, didn't stress over looks, and cared only about who a person really was on the inside.

Over a two month period, he gradually eased her into phone sex, explaining how he would massage her shoulders, kiss her neck, caress her nipples, which made her moist between her legs. She discovered that she had a talent for this type of *safe sex* as well, and she regaled him with descriptions of all that she would do if they were together.

The calls usually ended with him masturbating, but she was too shy to do it on the phone, in the kitchen, with Mother not far away. Sometimes, to please him, she faked it. But once in bed, after reliving all of the sensual acts Devin said he would perform on her, after basking in attention she had never gotten from anyone, her solo orgasms were quite powerful.

He put pressure on her to meet. He was a freshman at Oregon State (how she still longed to go there). A day wasn't a day without talking to him on the chat line. They professed deep love, kissed over the phone. She drew bold handsome portraits of him in her notebook when bored in class. She frequently wrote their names in hearts with an arrow: *Devin & Destiny 4 Ever*.

Finally, more than six months after they first started talking, she confessed that her real name was Maddie. He promptly told her that his real name was Arvis. She added that she didn't look exactly like she first described. He said that he didn't either.

"So what do you really look like, Maddie?" asked Arvis.

How to describe her plain haircut, average breasts, chubby waist, wide hips, short legs? Most significantly, how would she describe her pizza face?

"Arvis, when it comes to love, looks shouldn't be important."

"You're so right, sweetheart."

Then he added with a laugh, "As long as you don't have some giant mole on your face."

Maddie assured him she did not.

They arranged to meet at a Mexican restaurant in Salem. Arvis had a car. Maddie took the bus. The night before their dinner, while completing a beautiful, silent orgasm in bed, she imagined them making perfect love in the back seat of his car. They had known each for over half a year, how could this make her a slut?

She hoped he had birth control.

Maddie was careful about getting ready, not wanting to alert Mother, who would be full of questions and suggestions, the basketball girls' party never a distant memory for either of them.

She changed clothes in the bus terminal ladies' room, stored her slacks and sweatshirt in a locker, donned a nice top with tight jeans. All of her jeans were tight lately, since she had been gradually putting on the freshman fifteen. She wanted to add cover up to her face, but it made her break out even worse.

He was there first. She saw him at a dark corner booth. He had reserved this particular booth and had described it to her perfectly. She took a deep breath, approached the table, extended her hand, and said, "I'm Maddie."

The perfect gentleman, he stood up and gently took her hand in his.

That was when the light from a restaurant lamp struck his face and Maddie noticed the largest, darkest mole she had ever seen, the size of a black checker, on the center of his forehead.

She quickly recovered and sat. She took one more look and noticed little pock holes in it, as if hairs had been plucked. She stopped looking. It didn't matter. She was here with Devin/Arvis, the man of her dreams.

She said, "So nice finally to meet you."

Their eyes met and she could feel the kinship, the attraction. They were certainly cut from similar cloth, but how nice to find each other.

"I've dreamt of this moment," said Arvis.

They conversed about school, the chat rooms, barely glancing at the menus, his mole seemingly shrinking in size as they laughed and exchanged stories, not an awkward moment between them.

A waitress eventually took their order. Arvis excused himself to use the rest room. The appetizers arrived before he came back. Maddie picked at her nachos. She elongated her neck to see if he was coming back from the bathroom. When the main courses arrived, she got up from the booth and walked to the rear of the restaurant. She opened the door to the single occupancy men's room. Empty.

She scanned the restaurant one more time before officially acknowledging that she had been ditched by someone who had professed the deepest of love for her, someone who had a birthmark that made every day Ash Wednesday.

At least one day there was a chance her acne would clear up.

She apologized profusely to the waitress, head down, wondering if the nearby patrons could glean the entire humiliating story. The elderly woman took pity on her and allowed her to pay only for the appetizers, which was all of the money she had after the expense of the roundtrip bus ticket.

In the back of the last bus from Salem to McCannville, she sat in silence, refusing to cry over the actions of someone as superficial as Arvis. She was comforted by the fact that Mother didn't know about the date and thus she would not have to give a recap;

that, on the chat line, she would never again reveal she was Maddie nor meet someone in person; and that, in the future, there would only be Destiny.

MOTEL

The deputy stands next to his boss in the motel lobby, obviously confused by Nokenge's Patty Hearst remark.

Still smarting from Maddie's slap, Nokenge says, "Wealthy heiress kidnapped in the early seventies by a political group. They kept her needy, and brainwashed her with their ideologies. Hearst eventually helped them rob a bank and served time in prison for it. Popularized awareness of the Stockholm Syndrome, a condition where captives become dependent on their captors, certainly for food and comfort, but they also start identifying with them and take on their views."

"Heavy shit," says the deputy.

"Maddie's the wild card. She risked a lot bolting with her own baby and it's hard to predict how far she'll go to protect their family of three."

"So she's Patty Hearst?"

"Certainly need to know if it's Jesse or Al who comes first."

Nokenge stares out the lobby window at the empty parking lot, the one car by room fifteen, the sun setting behind the building. He pulls out his cell phone. Hits speed dial.

Maddie answers.

"Talk to me as if we're discussing more supplies," says Nokenge.

Maddie looks nervously at Al. "We need more diapers."

Encouraged, Nokenge adds, "You're the mother, Maddie. You can end this peacefully."

"And some donuts for Al."

"When she's in the bathroom, or asleep, grab Jesse, slip outside to the motel lobby where I'll be waiting."

"Fast food chicken is fine for dinner."

"I promise no one will get hurt. Al won't stay behind without you. We'll treat everyone with kid gloves."

Al's annoyed the conversation lasts this long.

"I'm sorry, Mr. Nokenge, but you won't be allowed in the room again. Leave whatever you can outside the door. Goodbye."

Maddie hangs up.

Al nods approval.

Al goes to Jesse on her bed, crouches down. She moves her face from right to left, up, down, and Jesse's eyes follow. She leans forward and he reaches up to touch her nose, but she pulls back. He giggles uncontrollably. Full of pride, Al says, "He's going to be a great athlete."

Maddie says, "I think Nokenge can be trusted and I think he's really trying to help. Perhaps if we can get him to delineate exactly what's going to happen, maybe put something in writing, we can get out of this motel room."

"He's playing us every step of the way. You can't trust him or anyone out there. Right now we're still free, still have Jesse, and can do what we want with him. As soon as we give up the baby, nothing will ever be the same. As soon as we turn ourselves in, we're all *caught*."

Nokenge feels his first sense of optimism since arriving. Maddie played along with him on the phone! He sends the state trooper out for fast food chicken and fresh diapers, eager to follow up.

It's dark, inside the room and out, when Nokenge places a box of Popeye's chicken and a bag of fresh diapers at the door, knocks once, retreats back to the motel lobby.

Not long after, the door opens noiselessly and Maddie slips out, holds a swaddled Jesse tight to her chest. She looks down at the supplies. She takes a long look in the direction of the lit motel lobby. She walks past the provisions, towards the lobby. She stops at the Honda. Ducks down.

Al exits the room, careful to close the door without sound. She hunkers down as well, picks up the provisions, inches towards the Honda. Al cautiously opens the driver's door, quickly shuts off the interior light, gets in. Maddie gets in. Al puts a key in the ignition. Turns it. Nothing. Dead.

They're blinded by a spotlight.

"Nobody move!"

SWAT One emerges from the shadows, rifle pointed, opens the driver's side, jerks Al to the ground, his boot in her back.

Al squirms. "Don't ever fuckin' touch me!"

Nokenge sprints from the lobby.

SWAT Two reaches for Maddie's door. "Give me the baby."

She locks it. Stares wide-eyed out the window.

Jesse lets out a wail.

Nokenge arrives, out of breath, says through the glass, "This is your chance, Maddie. All of you will be safe."

"Don't listen to that lying piece of shit," barks Al from the ground.

"Shut the fuck up!" says her captor as he applies more pressure with his foot.

With a trembling hand, Maddie opens the Swiss Army Knife blade.

SWAT Two points his rifle at her head.

"Stand down!" orders Nokenge. The man takes a step back, lowers his weapon. Nokenge looks at SWAT One. "Let her up and don't say another word!"

He lifts Al to her feet, presses her face-first against the hood of the car.

Maddie unlocks the car, slowly steps out. She can't stop shaking.

"Maddie, please," says Nokenge. "Don't do anything crazy."

"My mother's crazy."

Al struggles and her captor shoves her back down.

"Leave her alone!" Maddie holds the fluttering knife near Jesse's throat,

SWAT One lets go.

"Maddie," says Nokenge, softly, holding back the urgency in his voice. "Let me take Jesse. You know I won't hurt him."

"Nooo…" wails Al.

The trembling is so bad that Maddie feels as if she might faint, or drop Jesse, or accidentally cut him. With an intense quiver in her voice, she says, "I will hurt the baby if you don't let all of us go back into the room."

The SWAT guys look at Nokenge, who looks at the knife by Jesse's throat. Nokenge nods his head, sadly.

The women quickly duck back into room fifteen, lock and chain the door behind them. They put on the lights. Maddie places Jesse on the bed, then flings the pointed end of the knife against the wall, just as Al had done earlier, as if it was burning her hand. It drops lamely on the bed. She bursts into tears. "Don't ever put me in that situation again!"

She collapses on the bed, buries her face in a pillow, releases deep sobs.

"Please don't cry," says Al. "You know I hate to see you cry. I'm so sorry. I just thought we might have a chance to finish what we started."

Awake, wide-eyed, Jesse stares at both of them.

"Look," says Al as she approaches the desk and picks up the Seroquel bottle. She pops two pills into her mouth, swallows them dry. "I'm taking my meds."

Maddie does her best to slow down her breathing, to hold back the flow of tears. She reaches into the plastic bag for a fresh diaper, takes out the changing mat from the knapsack, undoes Jesse's blanket, unsnaps and removes the onesie he has been wearing for almost twenty-four hours, and places his last clean one next to him on the bed. She removes the wet diaper. She cleans him gently with a baby wipe, then rubs some cream on his bottom, followed by some powder. Jesse gurgles and laughs. Al moves next to Maddie, watches everything with undivided attention. They both are over him, staring down at the love of their lives, their hearts bursting with tenderness.

His naked little body is perfect: beautifully shaped hands with their tiny pink nails, the silky dark hair, the fully symmetrical reddish mouth, the bright brown eyes, the cute little bow legs, the two faultless dots of nipples on his chest. Everything about him is flawless.

Except the distinct protrusion of a bulging left rib.

AL

Al and Wynn lay flat on their backs in the softball field grass, doing what they do best: stare at the night sky while sharing a joint. They had become friends. She had gone to all of his games and he had led the basketball team to their first post-season appearance in seven years. There was even talk that he might declare himself eligible for the NBA draft.

But tonight the pair were doing more than partying, they were celebrating.

Al had finally gotten her revenge on Crystal.

And Wynn had been there to witness it.

Senior Day, Crystal's last game, biggest crowd of the year. In her bat bag, sealed in a plastic bag, Al already had a paper towel soaked with fresh dog urine she had procured from the base of a tree in the local park. Coach had brought his own dog to the game, Groucho, an ugly pug with a surly disposition, who stayed in the dugout as their lucky charm. Al had been giving Groucho extra water since the first inning. During the bottom of the fifth inning, just before the final out, Al discreetly dabbed the urine soaked paper towel along Crystal's shin guard. Immediately after, Southwest Tech took the field.

Properly stoked, breeze coming from just the right direction, timing impeccable, Groucho came charging out of the dugout before the first pitch was thrown. To the great amusement of all the fans and both teams, except Crystal and Coach, before Crystal even realized what was going on, Groucho took a healthy piss all over Crystal's leg, drenching it.

The laughter rained down like giant hail stones. From third base, Al could see clearly the nuclear reddening of Crystal's face. The best part was that she was only able to change her shin guard and had to wear her wet softball pants for the rest of the inning in order to stay in the game.

It was the perfect ending to Crystal's softball career.

"A beautiful plan," said Wynn as he passed the joint back to Al and exhaled a deep toke. "You belong in the Revenge Hall of Fame."

"The best part is that I got her without being caught."

Wynn nodded knowingly. His whole life had been basketball, from camps, to school teams, to travel teams. Always a star, he had been allowed to coast through his education while barely learning a thing, getting away with petty theft, vandalism, and all-around raucous behavior usually inspired by heavy drinking and pot smoking with whoever his posse happened to be at the time. Al was sure he must have paid someone to take his SATs. Originally from Canada, he once made a stoned bet with her that there was a state called West Dakota. Al happily collected the half-ounce of weed she won. Wynn was easygoing, and not vindictive, perhaps another reason why he remained in the world of the *uncaught*.

"Isn't this the night you usually fuck Tiffany the homecoming queen?" asked Al.

"Yeah, but I wanted to celebrate that bitch Crystal's humiliation. It's not like Tiffany and I are going out anyway. She's steady with Buddy, the quarterback. Girls are way too much work. Honestly, I prefer a quick jerk and then onto the party. I'd much rather hang out with you."

Al did an abrupt exhale as she laughed and choked at the same time. "I'm going to take that as a compliment."

"You're my bud."

She knew it was true. And he was her bud. He had saved her from another damnation that awful night. He wouldn't tell a soul about Crystal and Groucho. He wanted nothing more from her than her company.

"If you cut your hair," added Wynn. "I'd hang out with you a lot more in public."

"Why do you think I don't cut it?"

They were off into a new round of titters.

At this moment, Al felt she would remember this day with great fondness: her sweet revenge on Crystal, feeling so comfortable with another human being.

But that was not the case.

Later, after leaving her alone on the outfield grass, Wynn went to Laredo to do some heavy drinking with his buddies, something he would never do around her.

When the stars weren't out, there was nothing darker than a two-lane Texas road. Returning in the early morning, Wynn nicked the bumper of a Semi coming the other way and his car spun into a utility pole. All survived, but Wynn's right leg was shattered and so was his basketball career.

It was Al who drove him home from the hospital.

She let him recuperate in her one-bedroom university apartment, paid for as part of her scholarship. He took to sobbing frequently and mostly got stoned and moped on the couch. He stopped going to class, which allowed Southwest to take away his scholarship, which meant he couldn't renew his student visa. The local booster, who had been giving him an illegal monthly stipend, pulled the plug on the cash.

Wynn did not want to go back to Canada. There was nothing there for him, just an overbearing, wealthy father who had doted on Wynn, bragged on Wynn, forgave much about Wynn, because he lived so vicariously through his son and his basketball career. But his father had always cautioned Wynn to curtail his partying, warning it would lead to the demise of his athletic future.

Wynn hated that his father was always right. His father hated that Wynn destroyed all of his vast potential and, in return, cut his son off completely, refusing even to take his phone calls.

"What are you going to do after college?" asked Wynn over the summer as they enjoyed their favorite past time, he on the couch, she sprawled on the floor. He could walk with crutches now, but rarely left the apartment.

"Would you believe me if I told you I had no idea?"

"Yes."

The joint was getting small and Al attached a metal roach clip to it.

"If I'm not high, I feel like shit," added Wynn. Al thought of saying she felt like shit whether high or not. "Everything always had a logical next step: party, high school basketball, party, college basketball, party, then the NBA and the biggest party of all."

"What was the step after pro ball?"

"If I didn't have enough money left to continue the party, I wanted to go out with one primo binge, like Nicolas Cage in *Leaving Las Vegas*."

"So now your mind's a blank?" Al rolled a new blunt.

"Like the color has been completely sucked out."

"I used to want to win the conference champion-ship. But now, thanks to your never-ending supply of weed, I can't even picture that."

"I feel sad all the time," said Wynn as he fired up the new joint. His chin and neck were starting to bulge with fat and his glorious dark hair was rapidly thinning. "I feel like if I went out and just shot a basketball there would be no pleasure in it anymore. I can't sleep. I try to imagine things anyway I want, short of my leg back to the way it used to be, even that my dad welcomed me back home, and I still can't picture anything good, anything better than just sitting here smoking with you."

"Welcome to my world," said Al.

"But you don't feel worthless. You still kick ass every time you step on the field. You're smart in school. You can do anything you want."

"There's nothing more I want to do but play ball and get high."

"Yeah." He sat up. "Play ball and get high. How fuckin' great is that?"

"Except I never particularly enjoyed playing ball."

"No way," said Wynn. "Then why do it?"

"Keeps me occupied."

He sat back, shook his head in amazement. "Somewhere along the line someone must have fucked you up good."

Al continued to smoke.

Then Wynn leaned forward again, as if he were having a revelation. "Well then tell me. What happens when you don't have softball anymore to keep you occupied?"

Al exhaled the pot through her nose and mouth. She laughed hysterically and then Wynn laughed with her when she said, "You stupid motherfucker. I end up just like you!"

A couple of months later, Wynn used his only phone call to ring her from jail.

She stood outside his cell. He was unshaven, hair long, belly huge. He reeked of alcohol and she kept her distance.

"You're in deep shit," said Al.

"Drunk and disorderly. They found out about the student visa. I'm going to be deported."

Al knew that sooner or later, because of the dark hole Wynn was descending into, it was only a matter of time before he became one of the *caught*.

"I called my dad," continued Wynn, "and he said not to dare darken his doorstep and that I was a stupid shit who threw my career away and I got what I deserve."

"Dads can be tough sometimes," said Al without emotion.

Wynn kept his distance at the back of the cell, knowing Al couldn't stand the smell of alcohol. He lowered his eyes to the floor and said, "Marry me."

She started to laugh, but quickly realized he was serious.

"I can't go back to Canada. I know I'm a loser, but it will be a helluva a lot worse to be a loser near my dad."

Al leaned against the wall opposite the cell, a good six feet from the bars. "Sometimes things are just tough, Wynn. Sometimes you just gotta suck it up and find a way."

"I'm trying to find a way. Deportation has been on my mind ever since the accident. It held me back. I'm gonna get clean. I met someone who has this tele-marketing company. You know I'm good at throwing bullshit."

"That I know."

"I just need a chance. I'm going to make something of myself then go back to Canada and tell my father 'fuck you.'"

"Okay," said Al.

"Really?"

She'd rather say *yes* now than deal with what would come next: the Pledge Night card.

"That's awesome," added Wynn.

"But you better get a job, you better stop drinking, you better continue to stay away from hard drugs, you better not fuck with my shit. Or you will be out the door forever."

"Promise," said Wynn, now looking to meet her eyes. "If you were closer and my breath was straight I'd kiss you."

"And, under no circumstances, no way, no how, will there ever be sex."

"You know me."

"That's why you're still around."

"You know, and I really mean this, you probably get a pretty bad rap around campus, but underneath all the bullshit I think is a very kind and caring person."

"I'll see about bail." She walked towards the exit.

"Hey!" She stopped. "Did it ever cross your mind to have kids?"

Al continued walking away. She could've said yes, because it did. She would like to have a child and pamper her with a room full of toys and stuffed animals. She would love a child with all of her being, with all of her heart, and protect her every step of the way. But if she responded, it might open up her past, which would lead to explaining that when she had moved in with her aunt her infection got so bad she finally had to see a gynecologist. Despite the gynecologist being a woman, Al had difficulty lying still, not bursting into tears, even spreading her legs. The doctor finally persuaded her to allow an examination. After she finally got Al into the stirrups, popped her head under the sheet, and looked inside — causing Al to tighten every muscle in her body — the doctor let out a short, painful moan. She told Al that she had a serious infection and would prescribe some antibiotics. She begged Al to detail her sexual history, but Al refused. She finally informed Al that she would never have children because there was way too much scar tissue covering a severely damaged uterus.

MADDIE

It didn't take Maddie long to realize something about five year olds: they were mostly beauty blind.

During her junior year, to fulfill the practical requirement for her major, she volunteered to be a student athletic trainer for a local, co-ed, pee wee soccer team. They definitely had an awareness of each other's clothes and hair, but there didn't seem to be any major judgment going on that had to do with looks. Why else would they high five her when they made a good play? make sure she got a cupcake when it was someone's birthday? treat her respectfully and with great appreciation, as if she was their doctor, when she applied a band aid or some ice?

Mother was another story.

Whether it was the Haldol, or the energetic social worker that had been assigned to Mother once she was released from the hospital, or that Maddie (always Madeline to Mother) had chosen to live at home and go to college, Mother was as stable as she had ever been.

But she still did not want to be touched, considered Maddie a germatoid, and liked to do stuff like pose frozen in a ladies' store window as if she were a mannequin. The social worker helped Mother get federal disability so money and medical bills were less of an issue, and, most significantly, got her a spot as a day resident at the local Senior Center where Mother was kept fully occupied with Bingo to pottery making. The staff knew not to push her, and let her get away with a lot, and complimented her often on her clothes and hair.

"You know you're the reason your father left me," said Mother, as Maddie waited with her for the Senior Center bus.

Maddie had heard this one before. It was used almost as often as why Maddie's physical appearance was the reason why she never had a boyfriend and was still a virgin.

"Was I really that much of a nuisance as a child?"

"No," said Mother as she dramatically tossed a scarf around her neck. "It was your pronounced influence on my figure."

Pee wee soccer practices and games were an oasis in the McCannville desert.

The coach was one of the mothers, Mrs. Muller. There was no assistant, so quite often Maddie was asked to fill in as goalie during a practice, or kick or toss a ball for a drill. Maddie didn't have one athletic bone in her body. Mrs. Muller knew this, but still went out of her way to include Maddie as part of the team.

Maddie thought life would really suck if it hadn't been for the kindness of some of the authority figures in her life.

On the last day of the season, Mrs. Muller organized a party after the game. They sat in a circle in front of the goalpost, Mrs. Muller cross-legged on one side, Maddie on the other, and shared juice and cake while celebrating a successful season. Boys and girls climbed in and out of Maddie's lap as she fed them cake, or wiped their mouths. She told them silly jokes and made funny faces and loved watching them laugh as they tried out a few hysterical expressions of their own.

The mothers and fathers hovered by the parking lot and eventually it was time to go home. Holding back tears, Maddie told everyone she would miss them and that she couldn't wait for next year. They all lined up to give her a hug and she was mesmerized by the joyous feeling of each little one pressed against her. Mrs. Muller was the last to leave and held the hand of her own daughter, Olivia.

Mrs. Muller said, "Thank you, Maddie for all of your wonderful efforts. You have a real talent for working with children."

Unused to compliments, Maddie eked out a soft, "Thank you."

Mother and daughter headed to the parking lot, but before they got there, Mrs. Muller bent down and whispered something to Olivia. The little girl, pigtails flying, came running back towards Maddie, leaped into her arms, gave her one more big hug.

Completely blind to the acne, Olivia also planted a big kiss on Maddie's cheek.

"I love you," burst from Maddie, her chest heaving, her emotions completely unchecked.

"I love you, too," said Olivia.

Olivia ran back to her mom, who scooped the child into her arms and held her tight as Olivia rested her head on Mrs. Muller's shoulders and scissored her legs around her mother's waist.

When Mrs. Muller planted her own kiss on Olivia's cheek, the tears that Maddie had kept inside began flowing down her blemished face.

Maddie realized that all of her life when she saw scenes like this, she had always looked on with deep envy, longing to be Olivia or whoever else was getting such loving care. But perhaps because she was getting so close to college graduation, or perhaps because the *adultness* of her role at home had never been so clearly defined, she realized that she had no chance to be Olivia anymore, someone guided expertly by her mother to do the proper thing, someone loved unconditionally.

But Maddie would not let herself be overcome with despair. If she could no longer be Olivia, she could still be Mrs. Muller, someone Maddie now envied, someone who took care of a child in the proper manner, someone who taught her baby how to be thoughtful, giving, and loving, someone who protected her child at all costs.

Someone who was worthy of being loved back.

MOTEL

Later that night a car pulls into the motel lot. The large neon sign by the entrance is dark and the sheriff, standing just below it, wards off any potential *guests*. But this car is official. After parking by the front lobby, out steps Peg Renahan, top aide to the governor of New Jersey: blond hair with severely angled bangs; skirt long and tight, like the lines around her face; in her fifties; the woman behind *the man*. She enters the office, catches Nokenge by surprise, and immediately announces, "The governor's not pleased at all!"

"Neither am I," says Nokenge. He's sitting on the couch with the young trooper he has taken under his wing, and the head of the SWAT team. On the coffee table in front of them is a hand-drawn map of the motel property. Nokenge points to the three circles he's marked on the map that surround room fifteen.

Not pleased with being ignored, Peg does a quick sweep of the table, knocking the map and a cup full of coffee to the floor. The trooper and the SWAT guy stand and move to a corner of the lobby. The deputy retreats to the back office where the motel manager has been sequestered.

"Well," says Peg. "What are you doing about it?"

Nokenge looks with disgust at the coffee-stained map on the floor. He says, "What the fuck do you think we're doing?"

"You've been here almost ten hours. The longer this goes on, the more potential for unfavorable publicity for the governor and the state. And you know damn well that the governor is not in a position to weather any more heat."

"Perhaps you'd like me to toss in a canister of tear gas?"

"Possibly."

"Are you aware of the potential damage when an infant is exposed to tear gas?"

"Look, let's not be adversarial here. We all want the same thing."

"Then let me do my job. The longer they're in there, the more uncomfortable, bored, and irritable they're going to get, which means they're more likely to negotiate. Anything else could lead to the unfavorable publicity you so subtly mentioned. And believe me, I know what unfavorable publicity can do."

Peg knows he had been a junior FBI man at Waco, had opposed the attack, but had no say. He had resigned his post shortly afterwards.

"As long as you understand that your career is on the line," she tells him. "As long as you're aware that if Jesse is fatally hurt, this has the potential to be the worst New Jersey child disaster since the Lindbergh baby kidnapping."

Nokenge takes a deep breath, then sits back on the couch. "Ask me if I give a shit about how this affects my career, or the fallout of unfavorable publicity. All I care about is that this thing ends safely for everyone."

Peg takes a step towards Nokenge. She asks quietly, but with serious intent, "Are you telling me you don't have a plan to rescue the baby even if it means taking out the other two?"

"I was discussing just that when I was so rudely interrupted."

"Sometimes," says Maddie, "people can't always have things exactly the way they want."

She lies on her motel bed. Jesse is asleep next to her. Al reclines on her own bed.

Al says, "You and I have never had it the way we want. What's wrong with finally doing everything in our power to achieve that?"

"But sometimes you have to accept that you've done everything and it still won't change."

Al props up on an elbow, looks over at Maddie and Jesse. "That's still the difference between you and me. If I hadn't come along, your whole adult life would've remained unchanged: bored, alone, tethered to your mother."

Maddie doesn't answer, but she knows Al is right.

"You do understand, Maddie." Al sits up now on the bed. Her voice is calm, but her conviction clear. "I won't accept shit from anybody. The one time I did, it ruined my life. And now, because of Jesse, you must understand that you can't accept it either."

They hear the loud rumble of several trucks. Maddie goes to the window, pulls back the curtain. She sees the first TV news truck pull into the gas station across the street, followed by a handful of others. Along the road, cars and SUVs are everywhere and the view is suddenly a sea of headlights and bright spotlights as reporters, photographers, TV cameramen, and curious bystanders exit their vehicles. The trooper and the sheriff struggle to keep them out of the motel parking lot. Maddie hears the loud buzz of helicopters overhead.

"Media's here," says Maddie, in a tone so pained it's as if she just got slapped in the face.

"Shit! Shit! Shit!" growls Al as she leaps from the bed and goes to the window.

"Fuck! Fuck! Fuck!" declares Nokenge as he peers out the lobby glass door.

Peg stands right behind him. She says, "It's time to think seriously about putting your take-out plan into action."

"Just don't forget our safety net," says Al, staring Maddie head-on with her patented death stare. "If we can't have Jesse, no one can."

PART TWO

(Two and a half years earlier)

CHAPTER ONE

At the beginning of the fall semester, Lancer's athletic director and head football coach, Fox Phelps, called a staff meeting. He was an imposing man, six feet four, shock of neatly combed white hair, three sport athlete in his day, still a legend in Oregon as a player and coach. He stood at the head of the long table in the conference room and addressed his coaches and staff.

"Our new athletic trainer is a graduate of our own Lancer College. Our new softball coach brings extensive division I playing experience to our humble NAIA institution. Ladies and gentleman…Maddie and Al."

He stepped aside. The pair stepped forward. Maddie's hair was beginning to turn gray. Mullet gone, Al's black hair was cut severely short and parted in the middle.

Maddie was embarrassed by the attention, but glad to find a job that allowed her to live at home. Sort of.

Al hated the attention, hated the haircut, hated that she had to do sports information reporting as well as coach, hated that she was coupled with this new assistant athletic trainer. She might have hung out forever with Wynn, her *husband*, after graduation, smoking, drifting from one dead end job to another in Laredo, just like he did, if her aunt hadn't called to relay that her father was out of prison, hoping to reconnect.

Not in this fucking century or any other!

So she had cut the hair, answered interview questions responsibly, left Wynn and his bags of weed behind, just to make sure her old man had nothing to smile about.

At least softball was something she was good at.

First day of fall practice Al just ran the girls: outfield sprints, around the bases, around the campus. They had a male coach before, an old guy who was part-time and taught English at Lancer. Lancer softball was the doormat of the conference.

The town park in Scranton had a better field than this college, the infield dirt here rough and thin, the outfield grass thick and scruffy. The scoreboard would've been just as appropriate for tee ball. It didn't take Al long to notice that football had an impeccable turf field, with state of the art lighting and bleachers.

Second day of practice the players just threw. Then she ran them some more. The team was an out-of-shape, sorry lot, half of them puking throughout the afternoon. The assistant athletic trainer had her hands full with several cases of dehydration and heat exhaustion.

The third day they fielded, then ran. At the end of the running, the fourteen girls and the team captain,

Josie, approached her at home plate, most of them wheezing and spitting.

Josie hesitated, a few teammates nodded encouragement. "Coach, are we ever going to bat, maybe scrimmage?"

Al looked Josie over, then surveyed the rest of the group, who would probably lose to her old Scranton travel team. She looked at the assistant trainer who was nearby, but avoided eye contact as she fumbled with ice bags and towels.

"You mean why are you running so much when Coach Old School let you do what you want?"

"We're just trying to say—"

"Is it *we* now, or just you the captain?"

With confidence draining as rapidly as the color in her face, Josie looked at the girls again. A few looked away. "I think I speak for the team when I say we want to win and do our best."

"How many games did you win last year?"

"None."

How Al missed playing. If someone gave her a hard time, they simply threw down after practice. She never really thought much about what makes a good coach, but she knew that kicking the shit out of Josie was not the appropriate thing to do.

"Well, Josie, since it's only you who seems to have a problem handling my practices, I'm going to have to ask you to turn in your gear and renounce your scholarship."

The girls let out collective groans of protest, but Al looked at each and every one of them.

"Anyone else have something to say?"

Not a peep.

"Dismissed."

The team slinked off. Josie, still stunned, tried to apologize, but Al said she was done. Despite the tears, Josie finally impressed Al when, just before walking away, Josie said, "Fuck you!"

Girls gone, Al gathered her gear in the dugout. The assistant athletic trainer finished loading the water, ice, and med kit into the golf cart. She kept her head down, moved in silence, seemingly willed herself to remain invisible.

"What's your name again?" asked Al.

"Maddie."

"Do you think I was too tough, Maddie?"

"I'm not a coach."

"Your opinion as an assistant athletic trainer?"

Maddie made eye contact with Coach Al for the very first time and liked that the coach returned the look and seemed genuinely interested in what Maddie had to say.

"I did help out with pee wee soccer, and the coach, Mrs. Muller, told me that if anyone misbehaves it's best to talk to them in private so the situation doesn't escalate."

"Mrs. Muller's pretty smart."

"Way smart."

"I just ain't that kind of coach."

"The girls can see that now."

"Exactly."

The next day, Fox Phelps called Al into his office and said, about as nice as he could, "Young lady, I know this is your first coaching job, and as I remarked at the staff meeting, we're thrilled to have someone with your playing background here at Lancer. But you can't just throw girls, I mean *women*, off the team, and you certainly can't take away their scholarships just like that."

"She challenged me in front of the team."

He stood up, smiled that same plastic smile he must use for parents, or for glad-handing boosters, if this backwater school had any boosters. He walked to the front of his desk, touched her shoulder, and she couldn't help flinching.

"I understand that a player, even the team captain, shouldn't publicly challenge the coach, but there are more suitable ways to handle this and less harsh forms of discipline."

"I need to know now," said Al. "Are you going to back me up or not?"

"Need to know now or what?" asked Fox, his tone suddenly similar to hers at the end of practice yesterday.

Visions of Wynn and Laredo kicked in and she checked herself. "I just want to know how it's going to be."

Fox was back behind his desk.

"This is how it's going to be."

She could tell that in the office and on the field he demanded the same loyalty Al wanted from her team, but there was something about him she didn't like.

"Josie is reinstated and you're going to apologize to the entire group this afternoon for your rush to judgment. Dismissed!"

He reached for his reading glasses, looked at some papers on his desk.

Al wasn't pleased with being overruled just like that, and was even more pissed to be sent off as if she were his waterboy. She stood up, exited the office.

On her way out, she realized that what she didn't like about Mr. Fox was that he reminded her too much of Mr. Bear.

CHAPTER TWO

Maddie liked that Coach Al talked to her as if she was a respected peer, even spared her some of the harshness that was common on most days. And it was definitely fun being in a winning team's dugout.

Maddie was pretty sure all of the girls hated Coach Al, but after the run-in with Josie, who was having her best year yet, the girls buckled down. Mrs. Muller got the most from the kids because they cherished receiving her affectionate approval. Lancer softball girls tried their hearts out to get any approval at all, which at best was a nod of the head. They were in the best shape of their lives and discovered a new-found confidence forged by the day in, day out repetition of the fundamentals.

Coach Al confided in her one day that she didn't have the imagination to come up with fancy strategies, complex practices, or creative ways to motivate. Her best bet was simply keeping everyone busy.

Their first overnight was late spring, at the conference championship in Seattle. Earlier in the day, Josie had hit a home run in the bottom of the seventh to propel them into the championship game tomorrow. The players had crowded around her at home plate, slapping her back, praising her monster shot. Al had remained in the dugout.

That night, after making sure all the girls were accounted for, a quick phone call home to check on Mother, Maddie retired to her motel room where Coach Al sat on her own bed, worked on the laptop, anguished over writing a press release for the Lancer website. Maddie tried to stay calm, but this was her very first night away from home, which also meant this was the first time she shared a motel room. She didn't know the protocol for sleeping attire, so she settled in bed with shorts, tee shirt, bra.

Maddie wanted to talk about tomorrow's game; she wanted to talk about anything, but Coach Al was throwing up the usual brick wall.

Maddie opened the romance novel she had brought along. Coach Al grabbed a donut.

"We're going to get along fine," said Coach Al, breaking the tension, "as long as you remember four things: stop calling me *Coach* Al, I don't sleep very well, don't touch my stuff, and don't touch me."

"Do you have a germ phobia?" Maddie asked. "My mother's like that."

"No."

"It's a real challenge living with her without touching."

"Maybe it's time to move out."

"Mother has mental challenges."

"Dad?"

"Long gone. You?"

Al went back to the laptop, switched over to email.

"Goddamn spam!" she yelped. "Who comes up with this shit? *Please her with donkey dick…launch your missile…butter her bread…yur erectile make her smile.* They can't even spell."

"No way," said Maddie. "I don't get those."

Maddie stood, peered over Al's shoulder, almost touching.

Al shot her a look.

Maddie hustled back to her own bed.

"Sorry, Coach Al. I mean Al."

Al shut down her laptop. "One thing you'll realize, if you haven't already, I'm fucked up."

She shut the lights. They both lay awake in the dark until Maddie couldn't help asking, "You excited about tomorrow?"

"I'm not the one playing."

"But it'll be so great for the team, for Lancer, even your coaching career."

"I'm not sure how long my coaching career will last. Fox despises me."

"It would help if you at least made eye contact when you see him at practice or in meetings."

"You know you're a lot less shy in the dark."

"I think you're right."

"Do you have a boyfriend?" Al asked.

"No."

"Girlfriend?"

"Of course not."

"Nothing wrong with that."

"My best friend in high school was gay. I'm just not used to talking about such things."

"Me neither."

"Do you have a boyfriend?" asked Maddie.

"No."

"Girlfriend?"

"Nope."

"Ever?"

"I'm asexual. Like a dandelion."

"I had a boyfriend once. Guy I met in a phone chat room."

"What happened?"

"You've seen my face."

"What's wrong with your face?"

"Acne."

"You have acne?"

"Are you serious?

"I don't lie."

In her best imitation of Al, Maddie said, "One thing you'll realize, if you haven't already, I'm socially inept."

"I'm that, too!"

"But you don't care!"

They both laughed.

Then Al asked, "Is this like a regular chat room or a sex chat room?"

"Depends."

"Did *you* talk about sex?"

"For awhile I was Destiny. Tall, leggy model who loves to ski and speaks with a slightly British accent."

"No way! Do the voice."

"It's embarrassing."

"Pretend you're on the phone."

"Touch me there. That's it. You make me so hot, *baby*."

They exploded into hysterics.

The next day Lancer won its first conference championship.

The van ride back totally rocked. Al actually let them pick the music on the radio.

In the Lancer parking lot, just before dismissing them, Josie stepped forward and said, "Coach, I know I speak for the whole team when I say *thank you*."

For a brief moment, Al looked flustered. Then she seemed prepared to speak and everyone thought she was finally going to say something nice. "I expect you all to work camps and play travel this summer and maybe next year we'll qualify for the NAIA championship. Maddie, would you like a ride home?"

The next day, Al was invited to meet Lancer's president. She arrived early, a little confused because the desk in the outer office was empty. She heard some giggles behind the door of his office, then the secretary came out, a woman in her late twenties, who adjusted her skirt and said, "The president will see you now."

Al stepped into the main office and quickly sat on a chair in front of his desk, a tactic she often used to avoid a handshake. He was about fifty, with slicked back salt and pepper hair and an expensive suit. A photo of him, his wife, and five kids rested on the desk. Al could smell the secretary's perfume.

"I just wanted to take this time to congratulate you, Coach Al. I've never seen a team turned around so quickly."

"Thank you."

"There will be a hundred dollar bonus in your paycheck."

"Thank you."

He seemed to think she had more to say. Al realized he had nothing else to say. She stood up, exited the room.

All would have been pretty good—the team won, she had some extra cash, she was laying off the pot, she had someone nice to talk to—if it wasn't for her end-of-the-year meeting with Fox Phelps.

He gave her a copy of her yearly evaluation and, with original in hand, reviewed it page by page. On a scale of one to five, five the best, she got ones on everything from *coaching knowledge* to *ability to get along with peers*. He explained that all of the marks added up to put her on probation.

Al knew that it wasn't easy to fire anyone these days and this was surely the groundwork for a future sue-free termination. She looked at Fox. He seemed to sum up every low mark with one simple sentence:

"You reinstated Josie, but never apologized to the team."

She signed his original copy, tossed it back on his desk, left the room.

The meeting was obviously a productive one for Fox. Not only had he laid the groundwork to go in any direction he wanted with Al, but he was able to let her know that no matter how many wins she got, how many championships she won, he could still get her.

She hated that.

And vowed to fix it.

CHAPTER THREE

Maddie was thrilled that Al had asked her to help out with the summer softball camp at Lancer. Maddie watched the older girls shag flies in the outfield, the younger girls bat against the ball machine. Players from the team supervised the drills. Al watched from the dugout, made sure everything ran like clockwork. Mother sat in the bleachers, umbrella in hand to shade the sun.

A girl of eight swung so hard she slipped on the dirt, scraped her knee, began to cry. Maddie got out her med kit, put on latex gloves, cleaned the wound, put on some antiseptic, and a bandage. The girl gave her a big hug. Maddie smiled towards the bleachers, catching Mother's eye, glad Mother saw her being competent. Mother turned away.

Al approached.

"Hope you don't mind that I brought my mother today," said Maddie. "She's a day resident at a Senior Center but they're at half-staff this week."

"If it wasn't for you, the kids would've quit a long time ago."

"You're the talented one. I'm just the *benevolent interpreter*."

They both laughed, echoing the easy intimacy from their first overnight.

Mother stared, not happy.

"Let me introduce you," said Maddie.

Maddie knew better than to touch Al's hand and lead her over.

At the bleachers, Maddie said, "Mother, this is Al, Lancer's softball coach and director of the summer camp."

Neither made a move to shake hands.

"May I ask," said Mother, "what your intentions are with my daughter?"

"Mother!" exclaimed Maddie.

"I was wondering the same thing about you."

"Al!" exclaimed Maddie.

Mother's face twitched.

Al walked away.

"Can't you see she's a lesbian?" whispered Mother. "Look how she walks. The short hair. She shouldn't be working with kids. Her name for God's sake."

"Her real name's Alice," replied Maddie. "And she's my only *friend*."

"Any normal girl would shorten it to Allie. Can't you see I'm trying to protect you from the *aberrance* of the world."

Maddie headed to the dugout to help supervise lunch.

The next morning, Mother refused to get out of bed, refused to take her meds. Reluctantly, Maddie called Al to say she needed the day off.

Maddie wished Al hadn't talked to Mother that way, but she also wished, just once, that Mother would be happy for her, that Mother would acknowledge that Maddie was doing something she was good at and appreciated for, that Maddie had a friend.

Maddie knew Mother was mentally ill, but sometimes Mother seemed to know exactly what she was doing.

"I've decided we're not Jewish anymore," said Mother from the bed.

"What do you mean?"

"Exactly what I just said."

"We've never been Jewish."

"Says who?"

"We've never done anything Jewish, talked about it, acknowledged it, or celebrated any of the holidays. I don't think I've ever even met someone who's Jewish."

"You have."

"Who?"

"Me."

"Mother, since when have you become Jewish?"

"Your father's not Jewish, but I am. Which, according to custom, makes you Jewish."

Mother's eyes drifted off and Maddie tried snapping her fingers to get her on track.

"My father wasn't Jewish," continued Mother, "but my mother was, which makes me Jewish."

Something about her tone made Maddie think this was more than just a confused rant.

"How come you never told me before?"

"What was the point?"

"So I knew something about my heritage."

"No one should be Jewish in Oregon. Unless you live in Portland."

"Why?"

"Because everyone will think you're cheap."

"I don't think that about Jews."

"How do you know if you never met one? I'm cheap. And so are you."

"I'm not. I just don't make much money."

"All of this doesn't matter because I've decided not to be Jewish anymore."

"So what's different now from how things have been all of these years?"

Mother went quiet. Rolled over in bed.

Nothing was different.

The next morning Mother refused to get out of bed again, declined her meds. Maddie knew this was going to be every day now. She called Al from the kitchen, said loud enough so Mother could hear, her voice cracking with emotion, that she wouldn't be able to work camp anymore.

Maddie hated bailing and knew it was no way to treat a friend, wondered if Al would still be her friend. And one more thought preyed on her deepest insecurities:

Did Maddie even know how to be one?

Mother strolled in, big smile on her face, and asked, "What's for breakfast?"

CHAPTER FOUR

"You'll be given a $1,000 per year raise, Coach Al," said Fox Phelps.

After being summoned to his office first day of the new semester, Al immediately went right for the chair, completely tight-lipped. Neither even remotely pretended that they didn't hate each other's guts.

"The softball field will get a new scoreboard," added Fox. "You've been relieved of all of your secondary duties as Assistant Sports Information Director and will only coach softball. All ratings in last year's evaluation will be changed to fives, the highest mark."

Fox stood, towered over Al in the chair and gave her a look that asked, "What the fuck is going on?"

Al would like to tell him.

How she had a lot of time on her hands after cancelling camp when Maddie dropped out because no way Al could manage those kids without her. How she had signed out one of the athletic department's video cameras and had waited in her car in the school's main parking lot. How one Friday she had watched the president leave in his car, followed by his secretary in hers. How Al had tailed them to a motel and got their

I.J. MILLER

kiss on tape and their entrance into one of the rooms, together. How Al had reviewed the tape with the Prez, assured him *discreet* was her middle name, but that there needed to be some changes at her workplace.

But she knew that the best way to remain *uncaught* was not to say a word.

It had to be enough to be in the company of Fox Phelps—the man who thought he controlled her destiny, the man who tried to demonstrate that he owned her and that she could do nothing about it—and show him how wrong he was.

So she simply grabbed the original of her new evaluation, signed it, tossed it at him just like she had done the first time, and headed for the door.

As she reached for the knob, she heard him say, "Coach Al."

She turned.

He stepped towards her, jaw jutting out, eyes zooming in like power drills.

"Make sure you return the department video camera you signed out."

Did he know?

She tried to remain blank in case he was fishing. But his follow-up glare instantly caused her hands to tremble, her knees to shake, and it took nearly all of her willpower not to pee her pants. His look revealed a full range of hate, frustration, and anger, his pupils burning holes in her body. She recognized the expression she had seen so often on her father's face, one that told her she was about to receive her just reward, one that she

112

saw the last time she was with him when she had held a knife to his throat and he seemed unfazed, knowing he was about to sodomize her.

CHAPTER FIVE

"I'm sorry," said Maddie.

"No, I'm sorry," replied Al.

They each lay in the dark, in their separate motel twin beds.

Al laughed.

"What's funny?"

"I haven't apologized to someone since I was eight years old."

"Well I shouldn't have quit camp like that, but Mother—"

"No problem. I needed a few weeks to get some personal things in order. I should've been more polite to her anyway. It's just that with some people I don't know how to be polite."

"Well I'm glad you took the team to this fall tournament in San Diego."

"I did it so I could be alone with you."

"Really?"

"So we could talk."

"You can talk to me anytime."

"I find it easier in motel rooms, in the dark."

"I'm glad we're here together."

"Any new Destiny stories?"

"Long gone."

"Did you actually get off on the phone? If I'm getting too personal, just tell me to *fuck off*."

"I don't like to curse," replied Maddie. "I've gotten off, but after I hung up. Sometimes I faked it because some guys expect you to, you know."

"Yeah, I know."

"Thought you were asexual?"

"Doesn't mean I haven't faked an orgasm."

"Is there anything in the world that makes you feel good, Al? Even when we're winning you look as if we're losing."

"Talk to me again like you would a guy on the chat line."

"Feel my kisses lover."

"Not Destiny's voice. Yours."

"Really?"

Al closed her eyes.

"Put your hands on my big firm breasts," said Maddie. "Do you want to squeeze them? I know you do. I'll let you. I like being here with you. You smell so sexy. Feel so hot. I just want to make you feel good."

"I want *you* to feel good, Maddie."

"Why?"

"You're the most honest person I know."

"Oh, Al."

There was a loud banging on the door.

Al jumped out of bed, angrily jerked open the door, ready to floor this late night intruder.

A large overweight man stood there. Clothes tattered. Hair wild. Beard unkempt. Face puffy.

"Who the fuck are you?" asked Al.

"Same old sweet disposition," warbled Wynn.

CHAPTER SIX

"How did you find me?" asked Al, in her kitchen, after sliding a breakfast plate of eggs and bacon in Wynn's direction. She hadn't been able deal with him when Maddie and the team were around, so she had rented him a room, which had given him a night to sleep it off, and had driven him back to Oregon in the team van. From her sour expression, the team had known not to ask.

"Al, even though Lance is a piss-ant school—"

"Lancer."

"You're all over the internet when you win a conference championship. And I saw your schedule. And I just happened to be in San Diego."

"Don't lie to me."

He dug into his eggs, using his fingers.

Al couldn't shake the chill creeping up her spine.

"You in trouble with the law?" she asked.

"Not anymore."

"You clean?"

"Getting there."

"Working?"

He shook his head.

"Place to live?"

He remained motionless. She knew what was coming. It was just a matter of how *temporary*.

"So how the hell have you been?" he asked.

"It's difficult to understand your mumbling."

Wynn tried to smile. His teeth were yellow and crooked.

"Fucking drugs," he said. "You know how it is."

"Alcohol?"

"Whatever the shit, it fucks with you."

"How have you even survived?"

"Moved to Vegas. Tripped on a restaurant floor. Rebroke the leg. Big insurance settlement."

"Tripped on purpose?"

He attacked the bacon.

"How long?" she asked.

"How long what?"

"You don't want to play games with me. How did you get to San Diego anyway?"

Wynn clenched his fist, stuck out his thumb, wagged it back and forth.

"You must be rock bottom to show up like this."

"Can't someone want to see an old friend? Can't someone want to visit his *wife*?"

The word was so painful that Al stood up and left the room.

"Sorry," Wynn called after her.

She entered the one bathroom, sat on the toilet, peed. Every cell in her body was disturbed.

She found him on the living room couch.

"I'll give you a week to dry out, but that's it."

"I'm no good without you, Al. You give me discipline, structure. You understand me." He coughed hard, several times, his chest full of phlegm. "It's only a matter of time before I get whacked by someone I pissed off, get thrown in jail again, or keel over from some disease."

"I have a decent life here. I don't want you to fuck it up. I don't want to fall into old habits. If I'm a gun always ready to go off, you're surely the trigger."

He blew his nose into the dirty sleeve of his shirt. He nodded his head. Seemed calmer, as if he had done all of his best negotiating and realized that this was the most he could get.

Al exhaled a sigh of relief.

But then he said the thing that had always remained unspoken, put into words what hung over them at these moments in the past, but Al usually gave in before he took it this far. But she had underestimated the addict who sat in her living room and before she could stop him he mumbled well enough for her to understand, "I did save you from the disgrace of a dozen guys cumming all over you."

He was a junkie who was so far gone, so desperate, that he was willing to risk what was left of their flimsy bond, one that was rooted in the past but had just been severed in the present. It made her sad because he knew this would happen and said it anyway.

He let his body fall sideways on the couch and closed his eyes. She went to her bedroom, leaving her new roommate alone to wallow in his own stink.

"You'll need to get a job," said Al the next day.

She had bought him new jeans and a flannel shirt. They were at the barber's and he was getting a shave and a haircut. He was almost recognizable without the beard.

"Part time?"

"Full time. Janitor. Cashier. I don't care if you have to wave people into a restaurant wearing a clown suit. You need something to keep you busy."

"I don't have concentration for shit like that."

"Because it's work, dimwad! And aside from basketball practice you haven't done a day in your life."

The barber spun him around and now Wynn faced Al, who sat in a chair.

"Dude, there's a gap in your story somewhere," said Al. "What happened to the money from the insurance settlement?"

"You remember the plan: one primo binge. The party lasted forever. But not long enough. I'm still here."

"Well as long as you're *here*, you're also joining a twelve-step program."

"That shit doesn't work for me either."

She closed her eyes, tried to remember the Wynn who went out of his way with any local kid who asked for his autograph, the baller who righteously decked the center of an opposing team after the guy undercut Southwest's point guard, the freshman who risked the ire of his peers and lost his chance to get into the most elite frat on campus just to help a stranger who had wailed like an animal.

"That shit doesn't work for you," said Al, "because they throw a great big mirror in front of your face and show you exactly who you are."

"Suppose I agree to keep the apartment clean, do the food shopping, cook, and do the laundry? That's like a live-in maid."

Now he was just a user, con artist, junkie, trying to add her to the scam list. How he scored his drugs, how he got laid after the accident, how he lived off other people for so long.

"You fucked up once, Wynn. Big time. Doesn't mean you have to be a loser for the rest of your life."

"Look who's talking."

She gripped the arms of her chair so tight her knuckles went white. He was lucky she didn't have the razor in her hand. She stalked over to him. Got in his face so close the barber immediately backed off.

"This is why I don't want you around. You aggravate me. I feel like slapping the shit out of you."

He knew that look. If he could've made a dash for the door he would've.

Al channeled her anger into making every word crystal clear.

"You always make sure people live up to their end. But it's *fuck you* when it's time to live up to yours. First time you turn up drunk or using, you're out. You must do everything I ask. Non-negotiable. It's time to be real or be gone."

She took a step back. Wynn finally breathed. Then nodded.

"Yeah, I've been a loser," she added, "but I'm trying really hard not to be. Because that would make every shithole man I know the winner."

CHAPTER SEVEN

"I don't go out to dinner very often," said Maddie.

Al and Maddie sat in Applebee's. Al had emailed Maddie and asked her if she would like to have dinner together.

Al noticed Maddie's nice slacks and turtleneck sweater. Al wore her usual khakis and black polo shirt.

"This isn't a date," said Al.

"I know."

"I needed to get out of the apartment."

"Yes, and, so…are you finally going to tell me about the guy sleeping on your couch?"

"My loser husband."

"What?"

"Only married him so he could get a green card."

"That was really nice of you."

"Since when have you known me to be nice?"

"I think that you're—"

"I owed him."

"Why?"

"Your burger's getting cold."

Al took a bite of her sandwich.

"I could see where he could be considered handsome," said Maddie.

"He was the campus stud. Until he moved in with me."

"Was he hard to resist under the same roof?"

"I think you know this, but I want to be sure. I have no desire to touch anyone, be touched, or have any kind of sex, male or female."

"Why?"

Al asked for the check.

It wasn't until February when Al was able to bring the team to another away tournament. Maddie and Al lay in their respective twin beds, in the dark, completely still. They hadn't talked much since dinner at Applebee's. There was an awkward silence until Maddie finally spoke up.

"I have to ask you something and please don't be mad."

Al remained silent.

"It's just us, Al. Alone in the dark. No one else around."

Al stared at the ceiling.

"We're friends, right? Friends are supposed to share. That's how they get closer."

Al barely seemed to breathe.

Maddie took a deep breath. "Does not wanting to have sex with anyone have something to do with having faked an orgasm?"

There was a long silence. Maddie waited patiently.

"When I was eight my father molested me," said Al, without emotion. "Then he raped me regularly until I was fifteen. I faked an orgasm sometimes to get him to end sooner. I once used a red pen to put dots on my inner thigh so he'd think I had a rash. I ran away from home."

"My God."

"Prior to that first night I knew happiness. I had the most vivid imagination. And then he made it so I couldn't picture anything. The only future I could see was pain from the next time he visited my room. The only creative thoughts I had centered around elaborate revenge. I came to understand that he had been grooming me my whole childhood, gaining my trust, nurturing me, somehow believing that he could pick up again with the life he had with my mom."

Silent tears beaded down Maddie's face in the dark.

"Glad you're not crying," said Al. "There's no bigger pity magnet than this shit. I hate pity."

"I can't imagine what you went through. But I do understand the power parents have to hurt their children."

"Your mother's a piece of work, isn't she?"

"I was more of a mom than she was. But it was nothing compared to what you went through."

"Ever lay a hand on you?"

"Just the opposite. She's mentally ill. I once complained I was hungry and she gave me a box of Ex-Lax and I got really sick."

"Does it make you not want to have kids?"

"I dream of it all the time. Tall, dark, handsome stranger taking me away from McCannville, giving me beautiful babies I adore, take care of, shower with all the love and happiness I didn't have."

"Nice."

"I take it you never thought of having children."

"I have. And I can't. Too much scar tissue. But I do want a kid, one who loves to play—stuffed animals, dolls, storybooks—with a mind that whisks her to exotic places and magical lands. I want to give her that. For her whole childhood. Then I'm sure she'd have a happy life."

"You know even if you adopted you would have to hold her, feed her, nurture her. Kids suffer without certain types of *attention*."

"I know it's a pipedream. About the only one I have aside from smashing Fox's face."

"You hate him that much?"

"Reminds me too much of my old man."

"He's okay. As long as he gets his way."

Al propped up on one elbow, said sarcastically, "Don't you just hate people like that?"

"Were you just trying to be funny?"

"I think so."

They laughed in unison.

"Maddie, that guy from the chat room is an asshole. You're beautiful."

Maddie stopped laughing.

"No one ever said that to me before, in person."

"Talk to me again like you did with him. You can even touch yourself if you want. I really like when you feel good."

"I will, baby. And while I do I'll tell you all of the wonderful things we're going to do...*together*."

Maddie and Al started having lunch together on most days. Maddie took to wearing the same loose khakis and baggy polos Al wore, only her shirts were usually pink or white. They still looked nothing alike, but could pass for sisters. They exited the school cafeteria one rainy day and ran into Fox. He stopped. He scrutinized them from head to toe as if they were two wayward souls who didn't belong in church.

"Is there a problem?" asked Al, fists clenching.

"Just trying to figure out if you both *shop* at the same store."

CHAPTER EIGHT

"I googled the word *happiness*," said Al from her motel bed.

It was their last away game before the conference championship.

"What did it say?" asked Maddie.

"Feeling or showing pleasure."

"Makes sense."

"Not to me. Then I googled *happiness* in a children's dictionary."

"And?"

"Warm feeling all over when you have a pleasant dream. I like that one."

"I want you to be happy," said Maddie.

"Would you adopt a baby if you don't find a husband?"

"If I had to. But there's something about actually giving life to another, connecting in such an amazing way."

"You'd be an awesome mother, Maddie."

"Mother warned me never to have children—the source of all misery—and that I wasn't mature enough or pretty enough to have my own."

"It's good I haven't seen her since camp."

"I would take such good care of a baby."

"Tell me."

"Pamper her. Make sure she always had clean clothes. Make sure she was never hungry. Even before she raised her hands to be picked up I would scoop her into my arms."

Al unconsciously touched her own belly.

"I would love her so much," continued Maddie, "that even when she got older and I couldn't stand being separated I would let her explore whatever she wanted, be independent, as long as she was safe, as long as she did what made her happy."

"You'd always know what's best for the baby."

"You'd love a baby, too."

"You think so?"

"You'd never hurt the baby."

"Rather cut off my arm."

"You'd do everything to make her happy."

"I'd want to. Really. But I'm so fucked up."

"You'd love the baby as if she were your own."

"I think I really would."

"You have a great capacity for kindness."

"You're the only one on the planet who thinks so."

"I felt invisible until I met you."

"Then you think the baby could love me back?"

"I'm sure of it. Despite all we've been through, there's so much about both of us worth loving."

Al's cell phone rang.

She picked it up.

"Hello."

She listened.

"No fuckin' way!"

She smashed it against the wall.

"Everything okay?" asked Maddie.

"Aunt says my father's in a Scranton hospice dying of prostate cancer and he wants to see me."

Al buried herself under the covers.

Maddie stared at the ceiling and listened.

No one slept that night.

Al tossed and turned, wrestled with the blanket, top sheet, and pillows as if fending off monsters. In the morning, Maddie saw all of the bedding on the floor except the fitted sheet, which was pulled from every corner of the mattress and underneath Al as she lay in a fetal position on this little island of fabric, her face a tortured mess, her eyes wide open and in deep pain.

"What can I do to help?" asked Maddie.

"I don't know if there's anyone who can do anything to help me," said Al.

CHAPTER NINE

Al couldn't sleep on the plane either and arrived in Scranton during the early evening, awake for over thirty-six hours, and took a cab straight to the hospice. Homes with peeling paint bordered the highway, rundown empty factories were visible in the valley, the decaying streets were full of potholes. All of it looked especially miserable after the pristine beauty of Oregon.

Al couldn't stop trembling.

The hospice was run by the Catholic church and a nun directed her to his room. Even though Al was prepared to see an aging dying man she was still floored when she came upon her father, asleep in his bed, thick black reading glasses on his face. He was a ninety year old version of a fifty year old man. The hair on his head was gone except for a few gray wisps. The thick animal fur on his arms had turned completely white. His cheeks were hollow and his face was riddled with deep fleshy lines you could lose a nickel in. His fingernails were cracked. His fleshy, sunken lips seemed to cover a toothless mouth. His body was curled under the white sheet into a miniature version of the man she remembered.

Al didn't know if the time in prison had started this turn for the worse, the additional years of excessive drinking, the isolation of returning to his home as a pedophile drowning in his own miserableness, or if it was simply the disease and the failed chemo and radiation that had turned Mr. Bear into a dying cub.

Over the bed, attached to the wall was a metal crucifix. Al called the nurse in and asked if she could remove it.

"Your father isn't Christian?"

"He's not anything."

She seemed confused.

"Jesus abandoned us both a long time ago."

The nurse stepped up on a chair, carefully removed Jesus from the wall, then exited.

The commotion awakened Al's father and his eyes blinked open. The blue in his irises was nearly transparent, faded into a wet glassy blankness.

"Who are you?" he asked.

"Who the fuck do you think?"

"Alice?"

She grimaced. His left hand began to tremble on top of the sheet. Al didn't know if he had a regular tremor, or if this was his reaction to her presence.

"My baby girl," he stammered.

"Spare me."

"I begged your aunt for years to tell me where you were."

"Hoping to finish the job?"

"I didn't deserve to go to jail."

"You deserved to be raped in jail. Were you? I hope so."

He looked at her strangely, as if trying to confirm that she was indeed his daughter.

"I don't have long to live."

He coughed. He looked at the cup of water on the night stand. He seemed too weak to reach for it. She grabbed it, held it near his mouth so he could suck through the straw. He seemed about to clasp his quivering hand over her shaky one, his flesh below the fingers laced with broken blue veins and fading brown spots. But before he could touch her, she flinched, letting go of the cup as if it were a piece of hot coal, and it dropped to his chest, wetting him. She placed it back on the night stand, but made no move to dry him.

"I'm guilty of being a drunk," he wheezed, "of being very lonely after losing a wife, of making very stupid decisions, evil decisions, I know that."

"You're guilty of obliterating my childhood and desecrating my soul."

Old man tears dribbled down his cheeks.

"There's a lot I don't remember."

"It hurts a lot. Please stop. Does that jar anything?"

"Any possible way before I die that you grant me some forgiveness?"

Al looked at the wall above his bed. A round discolored spot remained where the crucifix had hung. She remembered clearly the months leading up to her communion, when the priest and the nuns had emphasized the *beautiful power of forgiveness*.

133

Al peered down at this man who finally looked on the outside like he was on the inside: pathetic. But he was dying. And maybe he did deserve some compassion.

"I battled long and hard with this," she said, "but I'm glad I came."

"Yes."

He managed a wrinkly old man smile.

"If I didn't come," she added, "there would be a lot left unsaid."

"You don't know how many times I wish I knew where you were so I could say I'm sorry."

"It's important for me to let you know that I survived you. That you didn't destroy me. It has been difficult but I'm trying to make something of myself. I hope someday to start a family. And you can be sure that no one, no how, no way will ever get the chance to hurt my child!"

The intensity of her words caused him to turn away.

"But before I do any of it," she continued, "I realized it was necessary that I see you, that I let you know that despite the fact that you're dying and decrepit, despite the fact that forgiveness is important and could help avert the hell where you're surely going, I still believe with all of my heart that you're the world's biggest piece of shit!"

Her hand went back and she was about to smack him. He raised his quivering arms to protect himself. Her hand dropped to her side. But before leaving she took a moment to cough up a mouthful of phlegm and, with the precision of an all-star pitcher, reminiscent of the punishment he often ejaculated onto her, spit it squarely all over his face.

She fumbled with the keys to her own apartment. She had taken the first flight out of Pennsylvania that would bring her back to the Pacific Northwest. She hadn't slept in three days. Her last meal was on the road with the team. Her hands couldn't stop trembling. The image of her father's phlegm covered face rattled her brain. She was glad Wynn was out on his morning paper route. He had somehow managed to keep the job all this time. He attended regular A.A. meetings. But now she needed the place to herself.

It was not the case.

The strong, pungent marijuana smell immediately smacked her nostrils. She stormed into her bedroom and there he was, reclined on several pillows, eyes closed, placid expression on his face.

Blood pounded her temples. Her ears throbbed.

He clearly didn't expect her back so soon. He clearly was so buzzed, so immobilized by ecstatic pleasure that he had no idea that she was about to toss him out of the two-story window.

Instead he smiled broadly, his eyes opening to little slits, and held out the joint in her direction.

Instinctively, she took it from his hand.

He made room on the bed, curled up in the far corner, knowing he needed to leave enough room for them not to touch.

She reclined, toked deeply, and welcomed the soothing sensations streaming through her body, so natural for them both, so familiar to be doing this together.

Wynn smiled beatifically and said, "There's nothing closer to happiness than the perfect buzz."

She exhaled a long deep hit and said, "I've been so hoping there's more than that."

When Al opened her eyes, she was immediately overwhelmed by hunger. She wasn't sure how long she had slept, but it was dark outside and dark in the apartment. There was an empty baggie on her stomach, just a few marijuana seeds remaining. She made her way into the kitchen, turned on a light, immediately scarfed down four jelly donuts. She saw Wynn's prostrate form on the couch, dead to the world. She noticed a folded piece of paper had been slipped under the front door. She picked it up. Read it. Immediately called Maddie's home phone.

Her mother answered.

"May I speak to Maddie?"

"Is this the softball coach?"

"Yes."

Well, *Alice*, do you know what time it is?"

"My fuckin' name isn't Alice!"

"Well, young lady, and I use that term loosely, I will not stand for profanity and my daughter is asleep and I'm sure would not want to talk to someone so…*crass*."

"You're lucky I don't ride over there now and bitch slap you…skank!"

Al hung up.

Wynn stirred. He looked out the window and realized it was dark.

"Missed my A.A. meeting."

"Lot of fucking good that's going to do."

Al gorged on leftover fast food. Sent Wynn out for more pot. Took a long shower. Put drops in her eyes to get the red out so she wouldn't look like Wynn, and headed into practice the next day.

Maddie was there but they avoided looking at each other. Al was sure Maddie's mother must have given her an earful, but Al didn't know what to say.

She was a bundle of energy, unmerciful with the girls, running them through drills they hadn't done since pre-season. She wanted to keep them busy; she wanted to keep busy: pacing the dugout, hitting rapid-fire groundballs at her infielders.

Instead of the usual abrupt dismissal at the end, she had them huddle up. Al swayed back and forth, her eyes seemingly rolling in their sockets, making more eye contact with her players than she had all season. Her brain also moved at high speed. They began swaying with her, rhythmically, wildly. Maddie watched from the dugout, her mouth agape with astonishment.

"No one beats us this weekend!" roared Al.

"No, Ma'am!" the team responded.

"Do you want to know why?"

"Why?" they shouted.

Al turned suddenly and headed to the parking lot, leaving her players staring at each other in disbelief.

CHAPTER TEN

"Sorry I called your mother a skank," said Al.

Maddie had just finished the final room check, shut off the lights, got into bed.

"You can't just not show up for practice, not answer emails, texts, or phone calls, especially right before the conference championship when we're first seed. You look awful. Friends are supposed to confide in each other."

"I decided to go to Scranton to see my dad."

"I wish you told me."

"He was hoping for forgiveness before he kicks the bucket."

"Did you give it to him?"

"What do you think?"

"Sometimes it's worth saying even if you don't mean it."

"Sometimes it's never worth saying!" Al snapped.

Maddie winced.

"I understand now why you're so out of sorts," she whispered.

"Do you understand what it's like to run away not only to save your own life, but to avoid taking the life of another, which would've put me back in jail to rot?"

"You were in jail?"

"This is me, Maddie. I'm always *out of sorts*. Sometimes I'm just different around you. Juvenile detention."

"Now I've made it worse right before the conference championship."

"I'm only surprised *you* haven't bitch slapped your mother."

"I love my mother."

"Love or an unhealthy caretaker attachment?"

A brief hesitation. Then: "Fuck you!"

There was a moment of silence, each of them equally stunned. Then Al started laughing. Then Maddie started laughing. Al laughed so hard she began kicking her legs on the mattress, which kept Maddie going.

"That was actually fun!" squealed Maddie.

There was a bang on the wall. "Coach, we're trying to sleep!"

They lay tight-lipped for awhile, until Al, for the first time, mimicked Destiny's accent with, "I missed you so much, *baby*."

"I never stop thinking about you, *lover*."

"Touch yourself," said Al, in her own voice.

"I am, baby. Can't help it when I'm around you."

"For real this time, Maddie. Touch yourself just the way I would."

Maddie's shock gave way to a soft, sensuous moan that evolved into movement under the covers.

"Imagine it's my hand," said Al.

"Feels so good. Makes me want to kiss you."

"Touching your breasts. Your nipples. Between your legs. Feel me everywhere."

"I do."

Maddie quickened her pace.

"Do you see how good we are together?" asked Al.

"Yes."

"We're the only ones who make each other feel good."

"I never felt so connected."

"Let's have a baby."

Maddie's hand jerked away.

Al's words raced.

"We could pool our resources, share everything. We'd create such a happy home for her. And ourselves. We don't have to adopt. We can find a donor. You could carry the baby like you dreamed."

Maddie could barely breathe.

"Have to think about it."

"It's your mother, isn't it?"

"What would everyone say? I'm not married."

"Fuck everyone!"

"Shhh…"

The next day, Saturday, was the conference semifinals. If Lancer won, they played in the finals on Sunday. It was the bottom of the seventh, the opposing pitcher was throwing the game of her life, and Lancer was down 1-0, woman on first, no outs. From the third base coaching box, Al flashed Josie the sign to bunt, hoping to move the runner to second, playing to tie, since they were the home team and would always bat last.

Josie seemed unsure. Al flashed the sign again. The pitcher threw the ball down the middle. Josie hit a home run. Game over. Lancer was in the finals. The team swarmed Josie at home plate. Al walked slowly to the dugout.

After the on-field celebration was over, and the team shook hands with the opposition, the girls filtered into the dugout to gather their gear. Not everyone noticed right away. First it was Josie, then the other seniors, who stopped what they were doing and just stared at their coach who remained immobile on the far end of the dugout bench. Eventually everyone took notice and remained frozen in their spots, eyes to the ground.

Maddie seemed the most confused.

Once Al realized she had everyone's complete attention, she stood.

Her face was pure rage. The players were used to Al's variety of pissed-off expressions, but none had seen this one.

"Josie!" barked Al.

Josie didn't move, inert with fear, but the players parted and there was a clear path between captain and coach.

"What signal did I flash?"

Head down, Josie mumbled, "Coach, the ball was right where I like it."

Al moved closer. With even more venom, "I asked you what signal I flashed!"

Josie was near tears and began mumbling wildly, "I'm a terrible bunter. I knew the pitcher didn't want to walk two in a row and would throw one down the middle."

Al was just a few feet from her.

"I got confused," added Josie in final desperation. "I thought you wanted me to swing away."

"I hate being disobeyed!" screamed Al. "And I hate liars!"

Al lunged towards Josie, while pulling her arm back at the same time, about to deliver a crisp slap to the face. Maddie, without thinking, reached out and firmly grasped Al's wrist.

With a nasty tug, Al jerked her arm out of Maddie's grip and turned towards her.

"How dare you touch me! Don't *ever* touch me!"

Maddie convulsed into tears.

The team stared with stunned expressions.

Al turned abruptly and left the dugout.

That night, Maddie was so shaken that she grabbed her stuff and slept on the floor of Josie's room.

Al stayed up all night, full of loathing for this job, for the weakness of her players, for the betrayal of someone she had shown vulnerability to. Al wished she could control these emotions, control her players better, have more command over Maddie so she would not humiliate her like that ever again and simply do as she asked.

But mostly she could not sleep because of a distinct and bitter sense of being the world's second biggest piece of shit.

The next day, in the finals, the players, in their own way, tried as hard as they could, but something had been stolen from them: a reason to play, a force of will to win. They got crushed 7-0 to a team they had beaten four times this past season.

Only stone-cold silence on the van ride home.

No one was as subdued as Al. Her lack of movement, her quietness, her blankness, her completely void-of-feeling expression was as if the pall of death had spread over her.

When she got to her apartment, Wynn, stoned, looked up from the couch, and said, "Your cell's still broken? Your aunt couldn't get through called here left message that your father died."

Not a facial twitch, a bodily flinch, or an out-of-the-ordinary blink of the eyes. Al just headed towards her bed, followed by Wynn, who rolled a new one to get them started.

They spent the rest of the night in silence, mesmerized by the orange glow from their continual deep tokes, lost in the haze of smoke that hung in the bedroom like a dark storm cloud, welcoming the dull disconnect of marijuana flowing through their veins, severing all severe emotions and massaging the mind into a muted tolerance of all that was painful.

CHAPTER ELEVEN

The fog from her all-night Sunday binge with Wynn lasted through Monday. On Tuesday, Al checked her emails.

Fox Phelps wanted to meet.

If Al didn't have the goods on the Prez, she would be sure she was about to be fired, so it must be that Fox *officially* wanted to gloat over her failure.

She stepped into his office, as usual closed the door behind her, sat in the one chair in front of his desk. Fox got up, opened the door, murmured something to his secretary just outside the door, and returned to his desk, leaving the door open.

He got right to the point.

"It has come to my attention that you nearly struck one of your players in the dugout after Saturday's semifinal."

Al studied him, trying to ascertain exactly what he knew and where he was going.

"I was angry, but I didn't hit her. She ignored my bunt sign. It would be like you sending in a play and your quarterback running one of his own."

"I understand the nuances of softball, Coach Al," replied Fox, voice dripping with condescension. "But a complaint has been filed by someone from your team and it's my job to determine if this warrants a formal disciplinary hearing."

"No way I would ever hit one of my players," stated Al. Her tone was sharp, but she understood that she needed to say all of the right things.

"The team member—and this was supported by several of the girls—said you got in her face and your arm went back and you would've hit her if the athletic trainer hadn't restrained you."

"Maddie will corroborate that I had no intention of striking the player."

With a look that can only be described as *dirty*, Fox said, "I'm sure she will."

He stood up from behind his desk, walked slowly to the front of it, sat on the edge, right in front of Al, which meant his crotch was eye-level.

Al dug her nails into an open palm as she averted her eyes.

They didn't really pay her enough to be in this man's presence.

"During the same meeting with the players," added Fox, "it came up that you may be having an inappropriate relationship with Maddie, which is, as I'm sure you know, a violation of school policy."

Al jerked her eyes straight up to meet the stare of her nemesis.

Was he smiling?

"There's nothing inappropriate about my relationship with Maddie!" snapped Al.

Her fingers twitched on her lap.

Fox's piercing blue eyes looked down on her. He leaned forward so close his face was just inches from hers, his granite jaw nearly touching her mouth, his sour lunch breath pressed against her cheeks like mold on a wall, his scent and closeness recalling her darkest moments.

"They heard you two *copulating*."

She slapped him hard, delivering the full blow that was intended at the hospice, completing the follow through that had been aborted in the dugout.

The crispness of the sound echoed out into the hall.

It caused his head to snap, but his face remained impassive. He leaned away from her, fully seated on the desk again.

Now he smiled.

That was when Al knew she was in deep shit.

"Coach Al," he said, loud enough so the secretary could hear, "you have no right to strike your supervisor or use physical force at any time in the workplace. You will be informed of the date and time of your disciplinary hearing. Good day!"

He dismissed her with the back of his body, returned to the other side of the desk. She wanted to leap out of her chair, tackle him, maybe shove him against the window so he would be pierced by a thousand shards of glass. But she was too stunned to move.

The sonofabitch got her. He had bided his time, waited for the right moment, led her completely down

148

his designed path. No physical contact had been made in the dugout and any team complaints could be written off to the sting of losing and simple poor judgment on her part. No one could prove that her relationship with Maddie was inappropriate. But Fox had just captured her with an airtight case.

If her mind wasn't dulled from the pot she would've sidestepped this, understood that something was up when he had opened the office door.

Fuck Wynn!

Fuck the softball team!

And fuck you Fox Phelps!

She wanted to repeat that as she finally staggered to her feet, but she was too dazed. She quietly slinked out of the office.

It was plain to see that she had gotten her ass kicked by a Master of Revenge.

The President spared her a formal disciplinary hearing and called her to his office the next day. She wore her usual khakis and polo shirt. Fox was already there, sitting in a corner, face blank.

"I've always been willing to accommodate you," said the President, nervously glancing at the photo of his family. "But with this clear violation, no matter what, my hands are tied." He looked over at Fox. "Violence against your supervisor is a serious matter and there is a witness."

Even when the boss deserves it?

"However," added the President, "I've been able to appeal to Mr. Phelps's sense of humanity and believe a compromise can be reached."

She looked over at Fox. His expression remained stoic.

"You can tender your resignation or accept reassignment as the assistant facilities manager at a $3,000 per year pay reduction."

"The person who handles the garbage, mops the gym floor, cleans the bathrooms...the janitor?"

"We never use that term," replied the president.

He removed his glasses, looked over at Fox, smiled gratefully.

Fox nodded.

"You stupid shit," she wanted to blurt to the President. "You think *you* orchestrated this compromise? *He* exercised his humanity? This is really what he wants so he can continue to write sub-par evaluations, continue to subjugate me, continue to keep me around as a reminder of his greatest conquest."

And she was just another deep breath from telling them both to shove it, that she was packing up and moving on, but not before mailing a copy of a certain videotape to the local paper.

But she did not want to leave Maddie and her dream behind.

"I accept the reassignment."

Fox Phelps was either a truly vindictive soul, or had grossly underestimated her capabilities, because now she would also have the opportunity to make him regret this concession for the rest of his life.

CHAPTER TWELVE

Maddie and Mother ate breakfast. Mother finished reading the local paper, then tossed it on the table towards Maddie. "Are you finally ready to admit your *best friend* is a degenerate?"

Maddie picked up the paper, scanned the article about Al's reassignment. "It's a misunderstanding."

"*Everyone* seems to understand but you."

"We're not having this conversation."

"I specifically forbade you to see her again after that disgusting phone call."

"I'm an adult. You can't forbid me from seeing anyone."

"You're living in my apartment."

"I pay the rent."

"The lease is in my name."

"I don't give a crap."

"See what influence the coach is."

"I'm sorry," said Maddie.

"Apology accepted."

"But Al has influenced me, in a lot of positive ways."

Mother took out her compact and began powdering her nose.

"What would you think if I had a baby?" asked Maddie.

The compact dropped to Mother's lap.

"You're getting married and I don't even know his name?"

"I'm not getting married."

"Fornicating before marriage?"

"Mother, I've only had one date in my entire life and that was a disaster. No man wants me and my acne. My hair's turning white."

"I see your point."

For a second, Maddie sensed that some real satisfaction could be derived from a bitch slap.

"I want to raise a child and give her a great life."

"How can someone who's a virgin have a child?"

"There's been a lot of scientific advances with fertility."

"I'm too young to be a grandmother."

"For once can't you see this isn't about you?"

"Madeline," said Mother, forcefully, clearly flustered by Maddie's firm responses, "the church specifically forbids pregnancy out of wedlock."

"We're Jewish."

Garbled sounds escaped Mother's throat.

"How are you going to work, support us, and have a baby?" she asked.

"*If* I decide to do it, Al's offered to help financially and share some of the responsibilities."

Mother began pacing erratically, bumping into the chair, the couch, her arms folded defiantly across her chest.

"I knew you were under her spell. I warned you that any kind of sex would lead to no good."

"She's a *friend*, someone who needs me now more than ever."

"My own daughter a lesbo!"

"I'm not a lesbian."

Mother stopped suddenly, stared at her daughter.

"You said yourself no man would have you."

Maddie buried her face in her hands.

Mother gave her nose a final dramatic dab from the compact, left the apartment to meet the Senior Center shuttle bus.

CHAPTER THIRTEEN

"Thank you for agreeing to have dinner with me," said Al.

Maddie and Al were at Applebee's, their food in front of them.

"I admit I was devastated at the conference tournament," said Maddie, "especially your last words to me. But I know the visit with your dad set you—"

"He's dead."

"Oh my God!"

"And I've gotten back into smoking weed with Wynn. And I smacked Fox in the face."

"Let me speak to Fox, explain to him that your father died and you're under a lot of stress."

"I've never used my father as an excuse and I never will."

"I've been such a bad friend, not reaching out."

"I agreed to stay on as janitor because you are my friend."

"I'm really glad."

"You're the only one who makes me feel like a person."

"You don't know how much I look forward to our trips away."

"I still want to have a baby with you," said Al.

Maddie placed a hand on her chest, as if holding down her emotions.

"I thought a lot about your proposal. The joy of giving a child what she deserves, having my own flesh and blood love me back, having a trusted companion who respected me and made me feel good, finding something that has to do with my own happiness and independence."

"It took so much for me to open to you," said Al, "and now with all the shit that has gone down, I want it even more. I want to thrive with you and a family."

"I want to be a mom more than anything."

"I want her to be just like you."

"You're the only one who'd think that."

"You're the only one who doesn't think I'm an asshole."

"There's no way I can do this without you."

"Same here."

Maddie smoothed out her napkin, aligned her knife and fork.

"But I don't see it working unless you get some help."

"For what?"

"The way your moods swing, your potential for violence, the enduring pain you carry around is pretty serious. As fond as I am of you I can't see exposing a child to such, please forgive me for using this word, *erratic* behavior."

IMMACULATE CONCEPTION

"I have no problem dropping Wynn and the pot," said Al. "You give me all the motivation I need. And I'm sorry for all of the times I was hard on you, especially in the dugout. And I'm sorry for talking smack about your mother, though I can't help thinking you deserve better. But they tried that shit at Juvie and it didn't help."

"You have to want it to help."

Al looked out the restaurant window.

"Think about it," said Maddie. "Maybe there's a way to remove the weight off your shoulders. Maybe there's even medication that would help. It helped my mother."

"I'm not your mother!" barked Al.

Maddie lowered her eyes.

"Don't you want to be able to hold, touch, and love the baby?" whispered Maddie.

Al fell back in her chair as if she had received the same blow she had delivered to Fox. The waitress approached with more water, but quickly retreated when she saw both women's eyes welling with tears.

"Yes. More than anything. Yes."

CHAPTER FOURTEEN

The next morning, Al crawled out of bed, made her way into the living room, shook Wynn awake, and said, "The party's over."

"What?" mumbled Wynn from the couch.

She picked up the half-filled baggie of pot on the floor, walked it to the kitchen, and flushed it down the garbage disposal.

"Nooo!" cried Wynn.

"I need to get my shit together if I don't want to end up like you."

"What's wrong with me?"

"You had the makings of a good human being."

"And?"

"Too many wrong turns. And I don't know if the one you made here was good or bad but right now I don't give a shit because I have to get to work."

Wynn struggled to sit up. Not too long after Al and he had fallen off the wagon, he had lost his newspaper delivery job.

"All the old rules are back in place," added Al. "It's your choice if you want to fuck up or not."

"Only job left is garbageman."

"If I have to clean shit at Lancer, you can collect it in McCannville."

As always, she was on time, 7am. The *facilities manager* gave her a print out of that day's required tasks, mostly cleaning and trash hauling. Al was told that tomorrow there would be a special event in the gym and Al was responsible for laying a tarp over the floor and placing chairs into evenly constructed rows, then reversing the process once the event was over.

Al would no longer be able to have lunch with Maddie because Fox made sure Al's break was at the time Maddie did rehab with the athletes. He didn't have to release the story to the local paper either, one laced with his righteous quotes, but he clearly relished the opportunity to broaden her humiliation.

The placement of chairs in certain spots, then their removal, was a perfect way to keep busy.

Al's story in the local paper caused a minor stir on campus. Her new smartphone came in handy. Whenever she walked through the gym or around campus, she had the phone whipped out, buried in front of her face as if she were reading a message or email. This made it easy to avoid all eye contact with students, staff, and faculty as they walked by. Even Josie…who was on her way to workout and saw Al, made her way over with an apologetic expression, but Al smartphoned right past her.

Later, Al received an email from Josie saying that Josie would always be grateful for having been coached by Al.

There was a moment when Al allowed herself to think that maybe she actually had the makings of a decent coach.

Then she deleted the email.

"Why are you here?"

This was the first thing Dr. Drummond asked after Al lowered herself onto a couch opposite the chair where the doctor sat. The office looked like someone's plush living room.

Dr. Drummond was in her sixties and had an abundance of silver gray hair that was held up neatly in a tight bun with a turquoise clip. She wore a white peasant blouse adorned with a rainbow-colored vest. She had on a long flowing green skirt that covered everything but her blue Crocs.

"How come all the ex-hippies abandoned their communes to become shrinks in Oregon?" asked Al.

Dr. Drummond smiled, then repeated, "So why are you here?"

"Trouble sleeping."

"Have you tried pills?"

"I've used a more *medicinal* approach."

"Does it work?"

"Yes."

"So why are you here?"

Al didn't answer. She didn't want to be here. She couldn't afford to be here. But she had agreed to this initial consultation to appease Maddie.

"I read the article about you in the paper," said Dr. Drummond. "Why don't we start with what happened at work?"

"You mean the one planted by my asshole boss just to stick it to me again?"

"You don't like him?"

"Do foxes shit in the woods?"

Al leaned back in her chair, closed her eyes. She knew for sure she would never say a word about her childhood, but it couldn't hurt to talk about Fox Phelps.

She explained her history with him, how he had recently tricked her, but the more she talked the angrier she got, the deeper her voice became, and the faster she spoke. She ended up breaking into a full sweat while finishing with, "But that motherfucker doesn't know who he's messing with. Just biding my time, making sure I don't get *caught* again."

Perhaps it *would* make her feel better if she could at least get someone else to agree he was an asshole.

"So you're here to work on some anger management and find a more even emotional keel?" asked Dr. Drummond.

Al let out an exasperated sigh.

"I'm here because my friend insisted as a condition for having a baby."

"Wonderful. Tell me more about that."

She really seemed to want to know and it *was* wonderful, the only wonderful thing in her life, and Maddie really was special. Al's voice became more animated and the words flowed quickly and easily, as she related bits and pieces of their story with some hint of their motel life. She really liked that Dr. D seemed completely non-judgmental even after it became obvious that Al's *friend* was a woman and that they really hoped to give a child the glorious life they never had, together.

"Tell me more about the childhood you wish you had," said Dr. Drummond.

"Time to go."

Al stood up.

"Well I think we've made some progress. I recommend you see me once a week."

Al walked to the door. This was the last time she would see Dr. Drummond. She had fulfilled Maddie's request and sought help. There was nothing more this doctor could do. She could come five or six times a week but she would never get serious about *sharing*.

"Wait."

Al turned back. The doctor retreated to her desk, took out a pad, scribbled something, ripped off the sheet and extended it towards Al.

Al took the paper, looked at it, but couldn't read the handwriting.

"What's this?"

"A prescription for Seroquel."

"What's that for?"

"Bi-polar disorder."

CHAPTER FIFTEEN

Maddie waited in the passenger seat of Al's Honda in front of the CVS drugstore. Al entered the car, waved a stapled prescription bag, and said, "All filled."

"Are you going to take it?"

Al started the car.

When the woman doctor at the Salem fertility clinic finished examining Maddie, she proceeded to walk them through their insemination options in order of cheapest to most expensive, which corresponded directly to lowest to highest percentage of success, all of it done at Maddie's ideal time of the month:

--Self-insemination of donor sperm.

--Intrauterine insemination of donor sperm directly through the cervix, into the uterus, and done at the clinic.

--In vitro insemination where they extracted Maddie's eggs, injected the sperm, then returned the fertilized egg.

The doctor suggested taking the fertility drug Clomid to stimulate ovulation.

"Will insurance cover anything?" asked Al.

"We checked her policy and it does cover portions of the insemination, but not medication or the acquisition or storage of sperm."

"I have $2,000 in the bank," said Maddie.

"My aunt offered to lend me money," said Al.

"Which brings us to donor options," said the doctor.

She laid out cheapest to most expensive:

--Friend donation unwashed.

--Friend donation washed.

--Anonymous donor sperm from a cryobank.

--Sperm from a cryobank that came with the life history of the donor, from profession to physical description to religion to some genetic history.

It was a lot to handle in one day, and all the baby talk had them both buzzed as they headed home from Salem.

"If I do really become pregnant," said Maddie, "I think it's best we live together."

"That would be amazing,"

"They have space in the Senior Center for Mother to live full time."

"Have you told her?"

"If I become pregnant."

"You can move in with me."

"What about Wynn?"

"No way he won't break the rules soon and be on his way."

"I feel bad putting him out."

"He's a loser, pothead, and a drunk. Used the one night he stood up for me to make me his bitch. He'll say anything, do anything to avoid helping himself and to earn a free ride. Having him around is a lifetime pass to a ball and chain. What kind of shitty influence would that be on a child?

"I understand."

"I'm in favor of in vitro."

"It's expensive."

"Best chance for success. Ultimately saves us money if we don't have to keep trying."

"Yes, coach." Maddie smiled.

"But what I'm most concerned about is the donor. Whether we go with an unknown or an anonymous life history, what guarantees he isn't a rapist?"

"Al."

"I have full confidence in your influence and the love you'll give the child, but what if it's a boy whose genetic core is exactly like his old man's?"

"Aren't you being a little extreme?"

"What kind of person jerks off for money in the first place? Everyone thought my father was a stand-up guy. We need to find a non-pedo/non-rapist who'll leave us the fuck alone."

CHAPTER SIXTEEN

Al sat on her living room couch. It was her day off. She had worked the whole weekend. Wynn was due home from his early morning garbageman shift. She had been watching him closely. His eyes weren't red. He didn't have the munchies. He made all of his meetings. His dirty clothes had no scent of marijuana.

She heard the garbage truck screech to a halt outside the apartment. They dropped him off because he didn't have a car. She turned on the TV, popped in a DVD.

Wynn entered the apartment wearing his gray work uniform. He went right to the kitchen for a Diet Coke, oblivious to the fake moans and dirty talk already emanating from *SLUT CHEERLEADERS*.

He entered the living room, stared at the football coach doing a cheerleader up against a locker, then took an astonished glance towards Al.

"Are you shitting me?"

She stared at the flower pot directly above the TV.

He sat down next to her, glared at the screen.

"Do you watch the cocks or the pussies?" he asked.

The quarterback had arrived onscreen and the trio were now involved in a threesome.

"Everyone always assumed you were gay," added Wynn, "but it's obvious you don't swing either way."

He picked up the remote, raised the volume.

She grimaced.

"Does this shit turn you on?" he asked.

"I'm very wet."

Wynn guffawed and Al had to smile.

"Does it turn *you* on?" she asked.

"You know I like cheerleaders, but it's been so fuckin' long."

"How long?"

"Probably not since one night in Vegas with a coked up hooker."

"I mean how *long*?"

Wynn smiled, looked down at his lap. "No one ever complained. At least when I was healthy."

The scene shifted to cheerleader practice and two girls going at it.

"I love girl on girl," murmured Wynn.

"I don't think I ever properly thanked your for saving me from frat zombies jerking off on me. You may be a douchebag, but you're a righteous one, and certainly no rapist."

"You're messing with my vibe."

"You can take it out if you like."

"What?"

Wynn leaned as close as he could without touching, sniffed, looked at her eyes.

"You using?"

"Pretend I'm not here."

"Al, you're freaking me out."

"Just don't expect me to touch it."

"I'm not sure it still works."

The movie soon moved into a gangbang involving the cheerleaders and the football team. The hollow sound of faked orgasms filled the room.

Wynn undid his jean button and the zipper, stuck his hand under his boxers, casually caressed his semi-flaccid penis, concentrated on the group sex.

Al continued to stare at the flower pot, tried to block out the flesh slapping, the inane dialogue, and the porn screams.

You can do this.

But her skin began to crawl.

"Damn it," he mouthed in frustration.

Maybe it was Al being there, maybe it was all the drugs and alcohol, maybe his equipment had passed its expiration date, but nothing was happening on Wynn's end.

Anticipating this, Al went to her bedroom, pretended to fumble around, then took out the condom that was already in her gym shorts' pocket.

She returned to the living room.

"If you put this on, I'll help."

"You'd touch it?"

"No. That's why I brought the condom."

Once she jerked his sperm into the condom she would make a quick exit to the bathroom, spill it into a pre-labeled sterile cup, and race it over to the clinic for storage until Maddie reached her peak time.

She wished she had smoked pot first, but Wynn would smell it on her and want some and that might affect his motility.

He was stiff enough so he was able to slide the condom on, but it was not very *form fitting*.

She took a deep breath, closed her eyes, and reached a shaky hand towards his penis.

"If it's this painful," said Wynn, "you don't have to."

"Been a long time for me as well."

She started jerking him off.

The reality of what she was doing made her dizzy.

She should stop. Better to take a chance on anonymous sperm than have to do this.

But look at all Maddie would have to go through.

She stroked him harder. He closed his eyes as well, listening intently, concentrating on her touch as if blending it with the loud moans coming from the screen. She had to swallow to keep from retching on his lap.

He grew in size, but it all seemed so difficult. The action on the screen got heavier and louder but everything else was perfectly quiet, except for the increase of her heavy, squishy, piston-like fist thrusts up and down on his condom-covered penis, as if punching someone, something she wanted to do.

"You're hurting me!"

She jerked her hand away.

"I'm no good at this," said Al.

"Agreed."

She paused the DVD.

"Terrible idea," she added.

"No. I'm actually feeling horny. And it's been awhile since I felt even that."

"But it's not working."

"Let's fuck."

This time the bile welled all the way up her throat and she ran into the kitchen and spit into the sink.

"Am I really that disgusting?" asked Wynn.

"Just a little under the weather."

He started to remove the condom.

"Wait!"

She was so close to having the sperm she needed. Just imagine if she got it all today, got it to Salem, and had it ready for Maddie.

Al closed her eyes and envisioned a pregnant Maddie. Then she saw Maddie holding the baby up towards Al so Al could take in every detail of her tiny body. She would be theirs, completely. Both connected.

"What the fuck," she said.

Wynn was pleased, in his own deviant way probably thinking that this could be a lifetime pass for the couch.

Her thoughts bounced everywhere, the dizziness getting worse. She had to focus. She reached into the fridge for a slab of butter.

"I'll be with you in a minute, Wynn. You start the DVD again if you want."

She ran to the bathroom, dropped her gym shorts, slathered in as much butter as possible, a trick she had learned at far too young of an age.

When she returned, Wynn was well-focused on the movie, stroking again, condom still on.

Al waited next to him. If this didn't happen soon Al was going to dash out of the apartment and just keep running, even if she did have a vagina full of butter.

"We can only do it doggie style," she explained. "I, uh, this way we can both watch at the same time."

"My favorite position."

"Don't touch me with your hands either. Just get off, okay?"

"No problem. At least I don't think it's a problem. Who knows? You're no Vegas hooker."

"Is that a compliment?"

"Al, you're my best friend."

How sad was that, because right now she would prefer that he kick her in the stomach rather than do what he intended.

He stared hard at a cheerleader masturbating, but still wasn't firm enough.

"Do you want me to help?" she asked reluctantly.

"No way."

He closed his eyes, face twisting with a focus she hadn't seen since his days on the basketball court, probably conjuring up the many cheerleaders he had fucked for real.

And then finally he was there.

He opened his eyes, looked down, declared in full manly glory, "Yes!" as if he had just scored the winning basket.

She positioned herself on all fours in front of the TV.

She slid her gym shorts and underwear halfway down her legs, and even though he entered her slowly and did not go very deep, she still screamed.

"Sorry," said Wynn.

"Just go for it. Quickly."

Wynn was careful not to penetrate too deeply, perhaps afraid to her hurt even more. She was grateful that his belly and upper thighs didn't touch her, but there was still his penis, like a knife extending from him, stabbing, withdrawing, only to pierce again.

Despite being well-lubricated, the pain inside was massive: scar tissue being broken; muscle memory placing her soul in a vise that squeezed the life from her.

She heard his pleased grunts. Felt his sweat on her back. How could he possibly enjoy being inside her? She was thankful for the insulation of the condom. Perhaps the satisfaction for him was that it all was working, that it brought back a time when he was healthy.

She closed her eyes and without thought, by some pure deeply buried instinct, began to pray.

If your spirit prevails, Jesus. If all demons are expelled by this one final copulation blessed by the lord and we are given the pristine gift of a child then I will believe again.

She remembered the priest telling her how Jesus could take all of the hate and anger in the world and turn it into pure love.

And then it *was* as if some sort of spirit took hold. Wynn's painful thrusts in and out, as in her childhood, seemed filled with anger and hate. Yet she knew she needed to do now what she could not do then: drain all the loathing by diffusing the weapon, take all of that hell and turn it back into the heaven of a beautiful child, the child that once was, the child that Maddie and she could create.

And it truly felt as if the spirit would prevail, that Jesus might really cleanse her soul and make her pure again.

Except even God would not let her find peace, because as Wynn's penetration increased in tempo, as his grunts became more rhythmic, as cheerleaders cried out with bogus pleasure, as he struggled mightily but kept falling short of that final orgasmic plateau—the promised land—he felt compelled to enlist her help by asking:

"Who's your daddy?"

No he couldn't possibly have said that!

No he couldn't possibly want her to answer that!

But he kept repeating it over and over with more anger and force, which increased both the physical pain permeating her body and the mental anguish shredding her brain, clearly frustrated that he was so close and she would not respond, pounding her harder and deeper now, seemingly prepared to go on forever, wanting her final declaration of his ownership, the right he had to claim her by simply blowing his load into her vagina. Then with his mightiest shout and his deepest thrust yet, he asked his dark question one more time—which caused her lids to clamp down hard and squeeze her eyeballs into tender agony, her fingers and toes to curl and scratch and grip into the carpet as if she were a tigress bracing against a male attacker—until she finally had no choice but to end this suffering by screaming back:

"YOU ARE MY DADDY!"

And with that he climaxed, soon pulling out, and she collapsed face first into the rug.

What was dizziness before turned into full-fledged vertigo, as if she had been tossed off a plane, cast out into the stratosphere, spinning mightily, her whole world upside down.

She howled like a dying dog. The communion words that had prophesized that first horrible night, rammed her brain again: *Lord, I am not worthy to receive you but only say the word and my soul shall be healed.*

No word, only Wynn asking, "Are you okay?"

His voice brought her back, somewhat, to the apartment, to the mouthful of carpet choking her breath, to the task at hand. She saw that he had removed the condom and thankfully had placed it onto the rug with the open side facing up, oozing with wet sperm that had been building for who knew how long.

With pure bulldog determination, she managed to reach for it.

"I'll throw it away," she sputtered.

She couldn't stand and just crawled to the bathroom, careful not to spill a drop, as Wynn stared with bewilderment.

In the bathroom, she called on all of her powers of concentration. Still on her knees, with shaking hands, she carefully spilled the semen into the sterile cup, careful not to touch the inside with her fingers, comforted by how heavy the load was that Wynn had produced.

She sealed the cup tight. She needed to get to Salem as soon as possible, but wasn't sure she could drive. She struggled to stand and finally, through pure force of will, was able to reach into the medicine cabinet. She twisted the cap off the pill bottle and, for the first time, downed a Seroquel. She took two, a double dose.

She stuffed the cup deep into the pocket of her gym shorts, which had never been completely removed during the fucking. She would keep it there, close to her own body heat as the doctor had suggested.

She headed to her car, Wynn anxiously calling after her, ignored. Though there were shimmering lights in her eyes, and still some dizziness, she commanded herself to drive, straight, true, and at the speed limit. The delay of a speeding ticket would diminish her chances for success.

She made it to the clinic, couldn't help running through the halls. Was she running? She handed a nurse the cup, who immediately dashed off to store it in their freezer.

Al held it together while receiving her receipt and returning to her car. In the parking lot, with her back against the driver's door, she collapsed down to the pavement, exhausted, lifeless.

Except for the tears that began to flow.

They exploded with a heavy thickness, the heavens opening, an overwhelming sense of weariness settling within her after she had done just about everything she could to bring about the full and final workings—if it happened—of what could only be described as a glorious miracle.

CHAPTER SEVENTEEN

And happen it did!

By the grace of something or someone, at the proper time of the month, Maddie's eggs were removed, Wynn's sperm was injected into an egg, then the egg was placed into her uterus, and by early summer Maddie was pregnant.

So amazing that they would soon have a family of their own!

They strolled the campus together all summer, whenever they could, unashamed, full of joy.

After the start of the new semester, shortly after Maddie's belly had popped just a bit, as they walked towards the gym entrance, Fox exited the building.

They both stiffened.

Fox's end-of-the-year evaluation of Al had been a masterpiece of denigration, though he was careful not to personalize anything, focusing only on specific issues that had, at best, ambiguous back-up. It was as if Al was the world's worst employee, a turd swimming in a bowl, who really didn't deserve to be at Lancer, but was here out of the goodness of Fox's heart.

It heated Al up even more because he gave Maddie her first sub-par evaluation as well, and no one worked harder than she did.

Fox stopped dead in his tracks, gave them more than his usual fundamentalist dirty look. He stared Maddie up and down, rested so hard on her tummy bulge, communicated so clearly how much he despised them both and all that they represented, that Maddie unconsciously took a half-step closer to Al, almost touching her.

"You two are not only an embarrassment to the community," said Fox, "but an abomination to the Lord."

A soft *oh* escaped Maddie's mouth.

Al bit her own bottom lip.

He brushed past them.

"Go fuck yourself!" spit Al.

Fox froze, turned around, nostrils flaring.

"What did you just say?"

Al was about to explain with her hands when Maddie whispered, "No. Please."

Al forced a stiff grin.

"I said to Maddie, 'Ever drive a truck yourself?' I'm thinking of giving her driving lessons."

Maddie tried but couldn't stop her giggles.

This caused Al to double over with laughter.

Fox stalked off, eyeballs ablaze with anger.

"He'll get his in due time," said Al.

"Hush. Let's focus on the positive. Like becoming roommates."

****

Al sat on the couch and waited for Wynn to come home from work. Since *SLUT CHEERLEADERS*, Wynn had become more like his addict self—reluctant to get out of bed, late for work, close to being fired again, weight ballooning—clearly assuming he didn't have to try as hard after what had transpired between them.

He walked in. She reached into her pocket, took out a half-empty baggie of weed, tossed it onto the coffee table.

He stopped cold in front of her.

"Haven't used since getting this job," he said. "Promise."

"I found this bag a couple of weeks ago under the couch. When it was full."

He rubbed his forehead, seemingly searching for some hasty negotiating plan.

"You never fully committed to A.A," added Al. "You're about to be fired from your job. Living with me isn't helping. Time to go."

He knew that non-negotiable tone in her voice. He plopped down next to her.

"This town is so fucking mundane anyway. If I didn't worry about you kicking my ass I would've binged a long time ago."

"Where will you go?"

"Vegas. My old man won't take my calls, emails, letters, texts. Cheapest place to live. Tired of these menial jobs."

"It's work, Wynn."

"Not cut out for it."

"Get your stuff. I'll take you to the bus station. Buy you a ticket."

"Give me the cash and I'll hitch."

"No way."

They sat silently for another moment. She had done more than pay off her debt to him. He had made it easy by breaking the rules.

He leaned in real close and said, "How about a farewell kiss for old time's sake?"

She glared at him as if he were out of his mind.

Then he burst into hysterics.

Al couldn't help laughing with him.

"Same old stupid shit," said Wynn.

"Agreed."

It was a scorcher of a day. The windows were open in the apartment, but no air seemed to move. Mother sat in a chair reading a magazine. Maddie dragged in the one old fan they owned and placed it on the coffee table so it blew in Mother's direction. She made her a glass of iced tea. Maddie could feel tingles throughout her body, as if her skin was glowing. Her breasts never felt this sensitive.

"In case you haven't noticed, I'm pregnant."

Mother, at mid-gulp, spat a stream of iced tea across the room.

"Oh, Lord, my daughter truly has blasphemed this house!"

Never a good sign when religion came up.

"Don't expect me to love it or care for it," continued Mother.

Maddie had prepared herself for one of Mother's diatribes and was keen on not being drawn in.

But Maddie couldn't help asking, in a tone heard so often inside these walls when as a girl she could not understand Mother's harsh rejections:

"Why? Please tell me why. It's my egg. I'm carrying it. It's as if I had a husband and we're going to have a baby and you'll be the grandmother and the circle of our family will continue."

Mother winced when Maddie said *grandmother*.

Then paced the floor frantically. Maddie thought it was good for her to burn off the frustrated energy. Then Mother sat. Now or never.

"I'm also moving in with Al next month."

Mother leaped to her feet. "Oh, my! Oh, my!" She frantically circled the room, grabbed her hair, determined to pull out fistfuls.

"Stay calm, Mother, we can get through this. I'm your daughter. I'll never abandon you. It's just time for me to grow up."

Mother picked up the phone, dialed 911.

"Come quick, this is a dire emergency!"

Maddie grabbed the phone and said into it, "I'm so sorry. There's no emergency." She hung up.

Mother took a hard look at Maddie, thrilled she was about to turn her daughter into a liar. She took one step towards the coffee table and stuck her right index finger into the fan.

Maddie screamed, leaped towards her. There was an instinctive pull-back by Mother once blade touched skin, but not enough to avoid a slice across the finger pad, causing blood to spurt everywhere.

Mother's eyes went dead, her face blank, head immobile. Maddie immediately rushed to the kitchen for a clean towel, wrapped the cut finger, applied pressure, elevated the hand.

Mother didn't recoil from Maddie's touch.

Maddie couldn't hold back the tears.

"I'm so sorry, Mother. I'm so sorry I never found the right way to please you, to make you happy. Please forgive me. I've tried. I've tried so hard. I love you. I really do. I love you with all of my heart and want to see you healthy and happy!"

"Then you're staying?"

A policeman pounded at the door. Maddie let him in.

"Everyone okay?"

"It's my mother," said Maddie. "She cut her finger in the fan. Can you give us a ride to the hospital?"

He looked at Maddie suspiciously.

"My mother's mentally ill. On medication. Having a rough day."

He looked at Mother.

Who smiled right at him.

"I'm so glad you're here," she said, with a flirtatious turn of the head. "My daughter was thinking of abandoning me."

In the emergency room waiting area, after giving the policeman a full statement about the finger in the fan, Maddie sat next to Mother, who was still smiling.

"We're waiting to see the doctor," said Maddie, "who will probably put in some stitches. Hopefully no nerves are damaged. I will also ask the doctor to examine you. If he determines that you're severely ill I'll ask him to send you back to the state hospital. If you can somehow get yourself together, then at the end of this month I'll pack up your things and move you into the Senior Center where I've already reserved a room, where I will visit you as often as I can."

Maddie looked carefully into Mother's eyes. Mother's smile disappeared.

With full resolve Maddie added: "As long as you respect me and my baby."

CHAPTER EIGHTEEN

"Cozy and private," said Maddie. "Just like our motel rooms. Only now every night."

They had just settled into their new twin beds inside Al's bedroom.

"Never thought I'd have something like this," said Al.

"It's a miracle."

"You look so beautiful with your tummy bulge."

"First time ever I almost feel beautiful."

"You must believe you are."

"No one can think I'm a loser again. A loser cannot be involved with a miracle."

"Our miracle."

"Yes," said Maddie, in a voice heavy with emotion, hormones airborne inside her. "*We* can spoil her in every way. She'll have discipline, but I want her to feel so loved that nothing bothers her. I want her to feel as if she has everything in the world she needs."

"Do you want to touch yourself?"

"Oh yes, lover," Maddie responded in her sexiest voice. "I feel closer to you than ever. Imagining my arms wrapped around you makes me tingle all over. Touch me, please."

"I am, Maddie. It's just you and me in here, safe from all the heartache outside, kissing you everywhere, running my hands all over your body. I can see it."

"I can *feel* it," said Maddie. "And it's fantastic."

The hormones landed and her tears began to flow.

"It feels like love to me," whispered Maddie. "It feels like you love me. It feels like the baby loves me. And I know for sure I love you both with all of my heart."

Maddie visited Mother at the Senior Center as often as she could. Al usually drove then waited in the car. Mother had her good days and bad days, but most visits usually started with Mother's arctic silence, which didn't stop Maddie from telling her about work, how the baby started kicking, even reading to her from the romance novels they both enjoyed, until Mother finally warmed up.

But today—maybe because the top Maddie wore was no longer loose enough to hide her tummy bulge— when she found Mother in the cafeteria next to several senior women eating their lunches, Mother said, to no one in particular, "There's my knocked-up daughter. No husband. Still a virgin. Lives with a lezzy."

Maddie tried to calm herself by believing that the residents were too old to understand, or probably thought it was just the deranged prattle of someone with Alzheimer's. But despite the fact the women quickly returned to their chili bowls, she was unable to fight off the same agonizing feeling of rejection she had experienced that Christmas Mother had tried to give her away, a rejection that had been repeated so many times, in various painful forms, and rendered her incapable of any other response aside from hurrying out of the room.

When Maddie got back to the car, it was a no-brainer for Al to read what was wrong.

"That bitch mouth off again?"

"It's nothing."

"It's something when an expectant mother looks so miserable. When a person's own mom can't be happy for her."

"She's not your average mother."

"I wouldn't know."

Al gunned the car out of the lot. They drove in silence all the way home.

Once Al pulled into their reserved space at the apartment complex, she couldn't contain herself.

"I forbid you to see your mother ever again!"

"I can't abandon her."

"Allowing her to bully you all these years is your business. But now it's mine!"

"Don't yell at me, please."

"Okay, but I'm not driving you anymore."

"Then teach me to drive."

Al didn't answer.

"Mother said I was too uncoordinated. But I want to learn. I want more independence."

Al looked at Maddie, then stared so intently at Maddie's belly it seemed as if she might reach out and touch it.

"To drive you have to be very safe and cautious."

"Are you saying I'm not?" asked Maddie.

"I don't like worrying about you."

"No confidence. Trying to control everything. Just like her!"

"Don't you ever!"

Maddie's floodgates opened.

"I'm always crying around you. I'm sorry. Ever since the Clomid. Though I don't think it's good that you make me cry."

"Get out of the car now!"

Maddie darted out the door, staggered into their building.

Al remained in the driver's seat for almost twenty minutes, hands squeezing the steering wheel, her erratic breathing the only sound piercing the silence.

She found Maddie on her bed, face down into the pillow, crying her heart out. Al sat on her own bed, stared at the person she cared about the most in the world, carrying the person who Al would die for rather than see any harm come to her.

With a quivering voice, Al whispered, "You know I'm an asshole."

"Just mean sometimes."

Maddie turned sideways so she could look directly at Al.

"Would you ever hit me?"

It was as if all motor coordination left Al, causing her to slip off the bed onto her knees and into a limp pile on the floor. Her elbows were forced to rest on Maddie's bed for support, so very close, but still not touching her partner.

"I swear I'd never ever hit you. Only wanted you to leave the car so I wouldn't yell anymore."

Their eyes met.

"I wish so much right now that I could reach out and hold you," murmured Al, "run my hands along your arms, make you feel better, make you understand what's in my heart and that I could never hurt you."

The only time Al had experienced Maddie's touch was when Maddie had grabbed her wrist in the dugout after the conference semifinals. It had caused Al's body to shake, her skin to tighten.

Nevertheless, Al willed herself to raise a trembling hand, move it forward until it hovered over the curved swelling of Maddie's tummy. Maddie's eyes widened with surprise. The hand lowered, so close, nearly touching, but then it froze, unable to go any farther. With a sudden jerk, the hand pulled back and slapped Al's own face, hard, causing a wince and a quick retreat to her bed.

"No!" cried Maddie, her hand reaching towards her companion but only able to grasp air. "Please. Don't ever do that."

Al sat, her head hung low, words laced with exhaustion.

"Sometimes, as we move along, as we get closer, I think I'm actually going to make it, actually going to have a handle on this and won't fall off the deep end. But times like these make me see I'm too fucked up."

Maddie sat up, dried her eyes with a tissue.

"Al, you're going to be a great parent. But I don't believe you've been seeing Dr. Drummond, or taking your meds. If you can't do it for your sake, or mine, at least do it for the baby's."

There was an urge within Al to lie. But Maddie knew her better than anyone ever had.

"The only way we can make this work, my love," added Maddie, "is if we both completely trust everything about the other."

CHAPTER NINETEEN

"Have you been taking your meds?" asked Dr. Drummond, who always made direct eye contact.

"Makes me sluggish and upsets my stomach," responded Al.

"Why did you stop seeing me?"

"Too painful."

"What brings you back?"

"Favor to my friend."

"That was last time. What about now?"

Al squirmed on the couch.

"Is your relationship with your friend—"

"*Maddie*," said Al, sharply, wishing her forty minutes were up.

"Is your relationship with Maddie sexual?"

"No."

"Just friends?"

"More than that."

"How would you describe it?"

"Partners."

"Life partners?"

"She's pregnant."

"Awesome."

Al could see that Dr. D was genuinely pleased.

"So you're life partners because you share in this baby in every way?"

"Yes." It was nice to hear someone say it.

"Do you prefer men when it comes to sex?"

"I don't prefer sex."

"Have you ever had it?"

Al didn't answer.

"If you could," continued Dr. D, "would you have sex with Maddie?"

Al lowered her eyes to the floor.

"I just wish I could touch her."

Al could hear Dr. D's deep breath. "You don't like touching her?"

"Don't like touching anyone."

"Why?"

Al remained motionless.

"What was your mother like?" Dr. Drummond asked.

"Don't remember."

"Father?"

"Trying to forget."

Silence. Al looked up, saw Dr. D writing in a notebook.

"Yeah, he raped me from eight to fifteen."

Al liked that Dr. D managed not to express sorrow or anguish, or say something stupid like, "I can't imagine how awful that must be."

Instead the doctor said, "Let me ask you again. If you could, would you want to be with Maddie in *every* way?"

"Everything seems like we're a couple and I do have romantic feelings, but I can't imagine anything beyond what we have."

"Do you think you love her?"

"I have a hard time defining my feelings using that word."

"Why?"

"Is there a name for this fear of touching?"

"*Haphephobia*. Sexual or physical abuse is a common cause."

"If I seriously took the Seroquel, would that enable me to touch Maddie and the baby?"

"It's important to take the medication, but it's not a magic pill that erases the past. There are four extreme emotions common with what you went through and important to let go of: *fear, anger, sadness, shame*."

"Sounds about right."

"The best scenario is to take the Seroquel regularly and come once a week."

"So we can talk about what my dad did and how it made me feel?"

"Yes."

"So you can help me realize that none of it was my fault and that I can't change anything now and if I let go it will take the power away from my old man and give it back to me?"

"You're a very bright young lady."

"Bright enough to know that my *fear, anger, sadness,* and *shame* run too deep. Aware enough to know that the entire process would re-open a cavity so large I would implode. Visiting my dad on his death bed almost destroyed me again. I can't risk experiencing more pain. I need to be strong for Maddie and the baby. It's my job to make sure the baby doesn't suffer extreme *fear, anger, sadness*, and *shame*. If we both do our job the baby will have a wonderful life and then maybe I'll be saved."

"You may be right."

"But how the fuck am I going to do it if I can't hold her, or Maddie?"

She wished she could cry. She had forced herself not to cry with her father. She would not show him weakness, would not allow him that victory, but all of the havoc had returned while squatting on all fours, her gym shorts and underwear wrenched halfway down as she called Wynn her *daddy*. But that day had been worth it. Maddie was going to have a baby and that was the most important thing in the world, even if Al was all cried out.

"It won't be easy," said Dr. D. "You have to really want to help yourself. You have to *participate fully* in the process."

Al stood and was about to exit.

"There's something else we can try." Al turned back. "If you're dead set against any traditional route."

Al looked at her. Dr. D didn't say anything, seemingly not going to until Al sat down again. Al sat.

"It's called Tapping Therapy, or Emotional Freedom Technique, a mixture of modern psychology and ancient Chinese acupressure."

Al knew there had to be some advantage to having an ex-hippie shrink.

Dr. D explained the ten tapping points on the body, from the top of the head, to below the eye socket, to along the pinky side of the hand. Depending on the spot, Al could tap repetitively with four fingers, or two fingers, or even the side of her hand. The doctor explained that the tapping was a physical way of realigning the thinking while going through a mental exercise that did the same thing.

"I won't have to talk about my father?"

"We'll just focus on you."

"Let's go for it."

As instructed, Al tapped each spot hard enough to feel the percussion, but not so hard as to make the spots tender. The doctor mimicked the taps for her so Al could follow along, devoting around ten seconds to each location before moving on.

Tap, tap, tap, using her fingers, Al knocked on her skull, different parts of her face, her collarbone, on the side of her chest, on the side of her hand, and repeated the process over and over. She found it soothing.

"Now repeat after me while you continue tapping," said Dr. D. "*I can let go of my fear.*"

"I can let go of my fear. I can let go of my fear."

Once a full tapping sequence was completed, Dr. D said, "*I can let go of my anger.*"

Al repeated it again and again as she tapped.

Dr. D: "*I can let go of my sadness.*"

Al tapped, echoed the words.

Dr. D: "*I can let go of my shame.*"

"I can let go of my shame…"

The doctor took her through the entire sequence again. The meaning of each sentence, the power of the words began to take hold. The tapping was a pressure that reinforced and embedded these thoughts into her consciousness. All of the repetition of phrases and percussion made certain imagery come alive.

There was so much *fear* the first night and every night.

Will tonight be the night he kills me?

There was so much *anger* after that.

Will tonight be the night I kill him?

There was so much *sadness* each time.

Why is Mommy not here?

There was so much *shame* hammered into her whether he came to her or not.

What have I done to be turned into such shit?

Al's body began to shake. She didn't see or feel Al, but saw and felt Alice, under him, the little girl lost.

And just as it was about to burst, Dr. Drummond—as the spirit had tried to do that sacred afternoon with Wynn—said, "Take all of those feelings and throw them away. Replace everything with *love*. Repeat as you tap: *I can be loved, I can love; I can be loved, I can love…*"

Al puked all over herself, on her lap, onto the carpet.

She wiped a trembling hand across her mouth.

"'I *love* you so much, baby girl,' that's what he said to me, every time, when he was done."

"How awful."

Al stood, her face scarlet with rage and disappointment, body still shaking, jeans streaked with vomit.

"If I can't *love* the baby and she can't *love* me back then what's the point of living?"

"It can't all go away at once. We've made wonderful progress. Sometimes it gets worse before it gets better."

"I can't handle it getting worse."

Al turned towards the vase full of delicate daffodils on the coffee table. She said, in a harsh tone, one matching the distorted expression on her face, "I have my own tapping therapy: *Fist to Face.*"

She punched the vase onto the floor, shattering the glass, scattering the flowers, soaking the carpet, deeply cutting her knuckles.

"It's the only way someone as fucked up as me can handle any physical contact. The only way I step back from the edge and avoid falling deeper into the pit."

For once, Dr. Drummond was speechless.

Al walked out of the office, truly for the last time, unconcerned about the mess she had left behind. She would tell Maddie anything she wanted to hear in the hope they avoided further conflict.

It was painfully obvious that the only chance for true redemption was in the power of the savior growing in Maddie's belly.

CHAPTER TWENTY

The fall semester was a careening, up and down ride on the Al roller coaster, who did her best to keep busy which seemed to be the only way to combat the anxiety that gnawed at her during each idle moment because there were so many damn things that could go wrong.

Maddie got bigger and bigger, soon waddling instead of walking, and Al drove her crazier and crazier.

Maddie was not to do any house cleaning or lifting.

Al would not let her eat fish or red meat, only high fiber, dairy, and fruits and vegetables.

Maddie had to be in bed by 10pm and take pre-natal vitamins. Once her ankles started to swell, Al insisted she wear nothing but loose sneakers.

Al finally gave in and tried to teach her to drive which was a total disaster because Al made Maddie so nervous she couldn't think straight. After that, Maddie had to sit in the back of the Honda at all times, away from the airbag.

Al obsessed over softball coaching jobs available in obscure parts of the country and how they should move and leave Fox Phelps and Maddie's mother behind. Maddie insisted she wasn't ready for that.

Al abstained from any *aural* sex, wanting to be sure Maddie didn't agitate the area.

Thank goodness for Lamaze class. Al warmed to the task, so familiar with mastering anything that had to do with basic fundamentals. Maddie worked on her breathing and Al was an excellent coach. A little too demanding at times, but Maddie needed her firmness to stay on task.

During an ultrasound the technician offered to tell them the sex of the baby. Al wanted to know so she could get past her disappointment if the child was male. Maddie declined.

"I don't care what sex the baby is. We will love the child with all of our hearts."

Finally, in February, Maddie's water broke. It was two in the morning, but Al was completely prepared, Maddie's spare clothes, toiletries, bathrobe, pajamas, and slippers pre-packed in an athletic bag. Al timed the contractions and when they were close enough together the doctor told her to bring Maddie in.

Al couldn't help speeding as they raced to the hospital in Salem. They hit a bump in the road and Maddie groaned then said, "Oh, my God, Al it's happening. The baby is going to come soon. I can feel it. We're going to be parents!"

"Stay calm, Maddie. It's great. I'm so happy, so excited. We deserve this. I know we do."

Maddie smiled.

Al had both hands on the steering wheel, complete concentration on the road. As much as Al liked to control everything, and Maddie too often yielded to Al's wishes, there was something about Al's reassurance that made Maddie feel as if things really would be all right, that during any moment of doubt, any bitter moment with Mother, having this baby was the right thing to do. Al had a certain strength and conviction that Maddie could only hope to have, and it was comforting, and it always made Maddie feel as if Al, ultimately, knew what was best for them both.

The obstetrician was already at the hospital, fully prepared. Maddie changed into a gown and they wheeled her into the delivery room. If a doctor, nurse, anyone would offer Al a few quick tokes of weed, she surely would've taken them up on it, but no, she needed all of her focus as a Lamaze coach.

The contractions became more frequent, Maddie's dilation even larger, and she was fitted into stirrups. The process began, the doctor encouraged Maddie to push, but also gave her the proper amount of rest. It wasn't a difficult birth, but it wasn't easy either. Al stood by the top of the bed, near Maddie's head, encouraging her to breathe, counting for her. The pain increased and Maddie became flushed with discomfort. Sweat poured from her scalp and dripped down her face. Her hands clenched and unclenched, palms open, as if they reached for Al. Al wanted to hold her hand so much, to bring comfort, support, but couldn't. If she had had time she would've tried some tapping on her own body, just to stay calm. If she didn't want to be razor sharp for whatever went down, she would've popped some Seroquel. Instead she reached for a clean towel beside the bed. She put it in Maddie's hand to squeeze, while Al squeezed the other end and encouraged her.

Maddie screamed, but lost none of her determination.

She was so fucking brave!

She was so fucking determined!

She was so fucking strong as she attacked this process with an energy and force Al had not seen before, eyes bulging, lips tight and puffy as she blasted out her deep breaths. This was her Maddie. This was why only Maddie could open Al the way she had, why Maddie was the only person in the world who Al would ever consider forming such a partnership with. At this moment Al believed she must feel some kind of love for her. She didn't want to say it, didn't want the sound of the word to upset the rhythm of this incredible moment, but she felt something. It must be *true* love—her childhood definition redefined—because it was a feeling that they were completely connected, as their hands were by the towel, and that Al never wanted to be anywhere else but by Maddie's side and that all goodness in life sprung forth from this special woman.

There was a final frenzy, last bits of forceful encouragement by the doctor, then Maddie shouted one more time, closed her eyes, and pushed as if her vagina was moving a mountain.

No, just a baby, crying instantly as its body braced against the chill of the room. A nurse grabbed the baby from the doctor. The doctor snipped the umbilical cord. With help from another nurse they quickly cleaned the baby. Al was too nervous to look. She watched Maddie's eyes, which followed every move of the nurse and the crying baby.

The obstetrician stood by them both and said, "He's a beautiful baby boy."

"Wonderful," gasped Maddie.

They had decided on the name Jesse either way, and Al realized she didn't care that he was a boy, she was so overjoyed he was alive, everything seemed normal, and their dream had become a reality.

The nurse held out Jesse in her direction and Al realized she wanted to give Al the baby to pass onto Maddie. Al looked at the blue fragileness of this dark-haired baby—so tiny, so delicate, more like an animated object—and turned deathly pale.

Al couldn't possibly touch him. Al couldn't possibly take a chance on hurting him, or tainting him in some way.

She lowered her eyes and stepped aside.

The nurse placed Jesse on Maddie's chest and Maddie held the child close, kissing the top of his head, copious tears spilling down her face.

And Al felt the tears, too, finally, only joyful this time, matching Maddie's intensity, rolling down her cheeks, as they welcomed their son, welcomed this beautiful promise of happiness.

CHAPTER TWENTY-ONE

"Nothing else exists for him except you and your boobies," said Al to Maddie. "You're a complete natural."

They were in their bedroom. A bassinet had been placed between the two beds, a changing table added to the living room where there was more space. He cooed and suckled on his mother's breast as she sat in a corner chair, Jesse blissfully changing nipples because he was so hungry.

"I hope one day you can hold him," said Maddie, "use the bottle, and help wean him off the breast."

"I would like that."

Al was content to stare, marveling each night when Jesse slept so contentedly, swaddled in his blanket, his little hands and fingers a complete marvel. Jesse had dark eyes and hair like Wynn, but otherwise Al could not see any specific resemblance. He didn't look much like Maddie either, his skin appearing even darker against her pale flesh.

"Do you want to grasp his pinky while he suckles?" asked Maddie. "He's starting to grip."

"Is it a strong grip?"

"Yes."

"Excellent."

Al remained motionless.

"Maybe when he gets bigger you'll realize he isn't so fragile."

"All children are fragile."

Maddie agreed.

"I think Dr. Drummond must be helping. You've been so calm lately."

"I can't wait to come home every day. So much to look forward to. I can't wait to see both of you."

"Our little family."

"I always knew family was important. Now I *feel* it."

"Time for Jesse to visit Grandma."

Al sucked in a gulp of air.

"She'll never accept him."

Jesse unclasped his lips from the nipple. Maddie held him straight up into the air.

"Just a tiny ball of love. That's what he is. How can anyone resist him?"

Maddie still had maternity leave left, but this past week she had brought Jesse in to meet everyone in the athletic department. Even the hardcore cynics had melted in his presence. Only Fox refused to come out of his office.

Al's eyes followed the baby wherever Maddie's hands took him. He was a hypnotic object that riveted her stare without mercy. Al had recently taken a picture of Jesse and emailed it to her aunt, thanking her once again for the loan. Her aunt was overjoyed. How great that Al had an association with something that made people happy.

"I'll take you tomorrow."

Maddie beamed. This was how she had envisioned life with a partner: ideas, discussions, harmonious mutual decisions.

"And I want you to come in with me," she added.

"You can't be serious."

"I know the two of you together could be toxic. But there's so much that's different now, about both of us. I don't want to hide you. I want Mother to see our entire family and how happy we are."

The next day Maddie was clearly nervous and Jesse seemed to pick up her edginess because he was fussy in the car. He had handled the infant car seat fine the few times he was out—visit to Lancer, doctor's appointments—but he didn't seem happy now. Maddie sat in the back with him and held his hand.

Al knew that the entire day would go that much more smoothly if Al could manage to keep her mouth shut. She focused on how cute Jesse looked in his tiny white knit hat.

Al parked as close as she could to the front entrance of the Senior Center. What a surprise in Oregon, it was raining. She followed mother and son from a few paces behind.

The Senior Center smelled like a combination of cleaning fluids and brittle flesh. Al was instantly reminded of her dad and the hospice. She couldn't wait to get this over with.

Mother was in her room, one shared with an elderly lady who had always welcomed Maddie warmly. Maddie was glad the roommate was in physical therapy and Mother was alone.

Mother didn't get up when she saw Maddie, which was typical. For a second, it didn't compute that Maddie had a baby. Mother also squinted her eyes at Al and then recognition finally set in.

Al stared hard, the same way she let a softball opponent know that if you opened your mouth it would be time to throw down.

Mother looked away, picked up a tabloid magazine, pretended to read even though it was upside down.

Maddie sat in the one wood chair. Al stood by the front wall, a good ten feet from everyone.

"Mother, this is Jesse. He's a big eater."

Mother looked at the baby, then over towards Al who was still giving her the death stare.

"You remember Al. My partner."

Al was glad to hear Maddie say this, glad she was here to witness it, glad Maddie thought it was important enough to share even though it was clear the mother despised everything about Al.

"Do you want to hold him?" asked Maddie.

Al took a step forward.

Maddie said to Al, "Don't worry, I won't let go."

This didn't stop Al's expression from darkening.

Mother's eyes moved back and forth from Jesse to Al like little darts.

"I don't want to touch him," said Mother. "He's a *germatoid* just like you."

It took all of Al's willpower not to finally deliver that bitch slap.

"Mother," said Maddie. "I understand if you don't want to touch him. But it's very important to me that you accept him and Al, that you accept our family."

Mother's roommate walked in, slowly, back hunched, leaning on her walker which had fuzzy yellow tennis balls on each of its four corners.

"Oh my!" she exclaimed. "You finally had the baby. He's beautiful. What's his name?"

"Don't touch him!" snapped Mother. "My daughter's a virgin yet she has a child. It's the work of the devil."

Their departure was hasty. Maddie fought hard to hold back the tears. She did not want to cry in front of Jesse. She held the baby tight.

Al couldn't get out of there fast enough and hoped no one stopped them or had anything to say because she might knock some old lady into her final resting place.

After Maddie got Jesse strapped into the infant car seat, Al was about to explode, about to tell Maddie that this was the worst fucking idea ever and when was Maddie going to realize that any contact Jesse had with that evil woman was going to be harmful to their child.

But Maddie looked Al in the eye and stopped the tirade before it started by saying, "I'm going back inside to tell Mother we're not coming back. I don't want her to wonder why I'm not visiting. I want her to know that if she rejects Jesse, rejects you, she rejects me. And ultimately that means I must reject her."

Al was speechless, marveling at Maddie's determination, knowing how attached she was to her mother, how she believed that her mother could not survive without Maddie, their co-dependence a complex burden for both of them. Yet Maddie was willing to let go, willing to be strong and sever this connection for the sake of the family.

Fucking amazing!

Maddie headed back to the Senior Center with strong resolute steps.

And just as Maddie marched through the sliding automatic doors, Jesse began to cry.

The sudden chill of the car? Strapped in too tight? The overall tension of the day? Being near his fucked up grandmother?

Or was it simply that he had yet to be left without Maddie?

"Stop, little boy," said Al, panic in her voice. "Mommy will be right back. Don't cry."

Al knew a crying baby was perfectly normal, but something about Jesse seemed to emote that he was in pain, or at least uncomfortable.

Al started the car, cranked up the heat. She took some keys off the chain, rested her knees on the driver's seat, faced Jesse, and dangled the keys to distract him.

He cried louder.

Al couldn't stand how his face got so red and his cheeks pruned up as if he were hurting and the tears drenched his face. She looked anxiously towards the main entrance, wondering why Maddie took so long.

Al turned and faced the steering wheel. She couldn't bear to watch Jesse cry. But she could hear him. A strong wail if there ever was one. It sounded like pain. It reminded her of the sounds she had emitted the night the frat boys had kidnapped her.

Al felt her own urge to cry. She looked back at the baby. With as soothing a tone as she could muster, she said, "Please, Jesse. Please stop. Don't cry. Everything's okay. Mommy will be back any minute. We love you, baby boy. We do. We're sorry you had to see that mean old lady. You won't ever have to again. Please. Please. I beg you. Stop crying."

But his wail became louder, clearly reacting to this first time he was calling to be held and his request was being denied.

Al got out of the car and went into the backseat. She got on her knees again. She wanted the baby to feel her presence. She was so close her breath bathed Jesse's cheek as she pleaded, "Stop. You're the best baby in the whole world. Everything will be okay. Mommy is coming soon."

Al knew this was going to happen one day. How was Maddie going to be around all of the time? She wished now with all of her heart that she had tried working harder with Dr. Drummond, that she had taken her Seroquel regularly.

Having her so close, yet receiving no comfort, made Jesse scream in a way Al had not heard before. He began to thrash his arms and legs, which must have hurt because he was so tightly strapped into the infant seat. Al was tempted to run inside and drag Maddie out, but she knew she couldn't leave this crying baby alone in the car, not for one single second.

Could the straps be cutting off Jesse's air?

Al's one simple job in this world was to make sure Jesse was always safe and now she was fucking it up.

But what if she hurt him in some way?

Almost out of body, as if she watched herself do it, she reached for the safety straps and clicked them open. He continued to scream. Without thinking, she placed one hand under each armpit and pulled baby Jesse out of the infant seat, fingers climbing up the back of his hair to support his thrashing head. She pulled him close, stepped out of the car, held him against her chest, bounced him the way she had seen Maddie do so many times.

Finally, Maddie came through the sliding doors. Maddie saw them both and she sensed that something was wrong and broke into a dash. Al wanted to streak towards her and hand off the child, but she was afraid to run with the baby so she continued to stand still, doing her little shake, whispering in her gentlest voice that everything was okay, that he was safe, that she would never let anyone hurt him, that she would always protect him.

And the crying stopped.

And Jesse cooed, then closed his eyes and rested his head peacefully against Al's chest.

There was an instinct within Maddie to reach immediately for the baby as she approached them. There was an urge within Al to extend the human bundle towards his mother. But they remained frozen. Until Maddie's right arm rose up, causing her partner to flinch, but Al could not stop Maddie because her own hands and arms were draped across Jesse. Maddie's right arm continued around Al's back, the other arm following around the other side until her hands clasped at the center of Al's shoulder blades. Maddie faced Al, their faces, their lips as close as they had ever been, breathing the same oxygen, her chest lightly touching Jesse, the bridge between them. She gently squeezed their bodies into a rich, rewarding family hug, as the joyous tears of the parents flowed freely, mixing with the rain; as the baby slept peacefully against his other mommy's chest; as they reveled in this moment of exquisite perfection, cherished this feeling of pure salvation, believed in the happiness created by this faultless trinity, all three overwhelmed by this untainted sweet moment of complete *love*.

CHAPTER TWENTY-TWO

The first time Maddie took Jesse for a stroll in a park nearby, she noticed a group of eight young moms sitting on connected park benches. Some seemed to be keeping an eye on young toddlers playing in the nearby playground. Others had carriages with infants wrapped as snugly as Jesse. Maddie was going to walk right by, but they waved her over.

They couldn't take their eyes off Jesse, *oohing* and *ahing*.

"Your son's so cute!" said a blond mother.

How Maddie loved hearing *your son*.

"Sit with us."

They made room. Maddie sat. One hand still gripping the carriage. She was so overwhelmed she could do nothing but listen as they continued chatting as if she was already a full member of the group, finally privy to some genuine *girl talk*, or at least *young mom talk*.

"Did you see last night's *Dancing with the Stars*?"

"Walmart's the best place for diapers in bulk."

"Hope that hot Dad comes by again today."

"Erin sleeps on her back, but I read the stomach is better."

It was clear to Maddie that no matter what you looked like, no matter how socially inept you were, once you had a baby, other moms accepted you.

Then one of them looked directly at her.

"Do you use the pump? I recommend it. Get some milk out so your husband can do a midnight feeding and you'll get more sleep."

And now they all looked at her. She felt their eyes slide down to the ringless fingers of her left hand. She felt the heat rush to her reddening cheeks.

"I haven't tried the pump," answered Maddie.

"Lucky you."

They all laughed until one of them commented on what a well-behaved infant Jesse was.

On the way home, Maddie realized she had no reason to be embarrassed. Single moms were fairly common these days. The mothers had even asked to exchange cell numbers.

Everything really was becoming perfect.

Al had started taking the Seroquel regularly, her disposition remained more even, and though Al had not touched Jesse or Maddie since that day in the Senior Center parking lot, Al recently said that she felt that someday soon she could change Jesse's diaper, which meant Al could finally stay alone with him.

Shortly after putting Jesse down in the bassinet for his nap, someone banged on their front door. Maddie opened it.

"Who are you?" asked a man.

"Who are you?" asked Maddie.

"Wynn."

That evening, after Al returned from work, they both stood over Wynn who was passed out on the couch. His clothes smelled. His breath reeked of alcohol. His cheeks were puffy. Hair wild.

Al slapped him across the face.

"Al!" shrieked Maddie.

Al trembled all over.

How dare he show up again!

How dare he show up drunk!

She needed to get him out of here before he discovered Jesse sleeping in the next room, though she highly doubted he could put two and two together, especially in his sorry state.

"Wake up, asshole. Time for you to hit the road."

"He can't even walk," said Maddie. "Let him stay the night."

Still dazed—by his inebriation and the blow to his face—Wynn managed to sit up.

"I gave him a chance last time, Maddie, but he fucked up. Told him never to come back. Bailed his sorry ass out too many times. He's an alcoholic and a junkie."

"Just an alcoholic now," mumbled Wynn. "Drugs too expensive."

"What are you doing here?" demanded Al.

"Shhh," said Maddie. "Jesse's—"

"What are you doing here?" repeated Al.

"I know I'm not welcome," sputtered Wynn. "But Vegas dried up and I got arrested for vagrancy and was ordered to leave town and my only chance is to go back to Vancouver, knock on my dad's door, plead for mercy."

"You fucked up sonofabitch, you still haven't answered my question."

Maddie started to interject, but Al gave her an ice pick look and Maddie knew to back off.

"Hitched west. Got a truck driver to take me north. Drop me off here. Need to crash for one night. I'll be back on the road tomorrow."

He passed out again, flopping on the couch like a lifeless mannequin.

This can't fucking be happening!

"Go in the other room," Al said to Maddie, her voice low, but firm. "Check on Jesse. Make sure he's okay. Keep him in there. I don't want him near this filth."

Maddie didn't understand why Al was so bent out of shape, but she knew very little about Al's history with Wynn. He appeared almost dead except for his loud snores. She left the room quietly.

Al punched Wynn as hard as she could in the arm. He yelped loudly. She grabbed a pillow to cover his mouth. He struggled. Al pressed down even harder. Her brain was in a whirl, thoughts speeding like they had before the Seroquel. Wynn was just a speck on this planet, connected to no one. He would not be missed. He needed to be completely out of their lives.

His struggling increased and she finally dropped the pillow to the ground.

"What the fuck?"

"You're lucky I don't kill you," said Al.

He forced himself to sit up.

"I know I should've cleaned up before coming but I had no place to stay tonight and I really am moving on tomorrow and I thought just one night."

The truck driver must have bought him a bottle to shut him up and Al was tempted to do the same thing.

But if she kept him drunk then how was she supposed to boot his sorry ass?

She went into the bedroom, said to Maddie, "I'll let him stay one night then put him on a bus to Vancouver. I'll call in sick tomorrow. I'll sleep in the living room tonight, keep an eye on him. You remain here."

Maddie looked at her, still confused by all the tense hoopla.

Al left the room. She grabbed a spare blanket, positioned herself in a chair directly opposite Wynn. She kept the lights on. She stared at his dirtiness, all his excess weight back, probably had lice or something. She would have the couch fumigated. She was not going to sleep tonight. She needed to stay awake and available for damage control. She was definitely going to find a job somewhere else before Maddie's maternity leave and vacation time were up, one that paid more so Maddie didn't have to work, one in a secluded part of the country where they could use fake names.

It was almost impossible to stay awake for an entire night in a chair, but Al's heart raced so hard, her thoughts banged so forcefully that she did manage to sit there and stare and hope that daylight came as soon as possible and that Wynn was at least sober enough to walk himself to the car.

She nodded off a little before dawn, but she probably wouldn't have been able to stop Wynn anyway as he lurched off the couch and staggered his way to the bathroom and began puking his guts into the toilet.

This woke Maddie, as well as Jesse, and he began to fuss. She picked him up and opened the bedroom door to make sure everything was okay. Wynn looked up and saw her and the baby by the bathroom entrance.

With more coherency than the previous night, he said, "Sorry to wake you. I didn't know you had a baby. What's its name?"

Al appeared, trying to play it cool, but not sure she was hiding her horror.

"Jesse," said Maddie.

Al closed the bathroom door and was alone with Wynn, who threw some water on his face.

Jesse was still fussing and needed a change. Maddie brought him to the changing table in the living room. Maddie laid Jesse down, unsnapped his onesie, removed the dirty diaper, and started cleaning him up.

As Wynn dried his face, Al studied him. He had definitely sobered up. No alarms seemed to be going off like *this must be why Al let me fuck her*! For all Wynn knew, Maddie could just be a roommate, brought in to share the rent.

Either way, she needed to get him out of here as soon as possible.

Without touching him, but by carefully positioning her body, she guided him out of the bathroom, into the living room, away from the couch, towards the front door.

"C'mon, Wynn, I'll buy you breakfast and put you on a bus to Vancouver." She tried to keep her tone light but it came out half-mean when she added, "I know I said no more handouts, but if it means never having to see your ugly face and saggy butt again it will be worth it."

Wynn took a step towards Maddie, looked over her shoulder while she completed the fastening of Jesse's new diaper. Jesse had stopped fussing and was smiling and cooing, reaching a finger into his mouth that he lightly sucked.

"He's really cute," said Wynn, seemingly trying to smooth over the great unease he had inspired. "Congratulations."

"Thank you," said Maddie, always the proud mother.

Al's eyes darted from Jesse to Wynn back to Jesse back to Wynn. She finally exhaled, or at least it seemed like it was the first complete breath since discovering Wynn on the couch yesterday evening. His brain was way too fried and this would be the last they would see of him.

But then Maddie pulled off the onesie completely so she could dress him in a fresh one and Wynn stared, suddenly focused, exhaling his own sharp breath.

"Holy shit!"

"What?" asked Maddie.

"What?" asked Al.

Wynn looked at Maddie. Then he looked at Jesse. Then he looked at Al, hard, studying her.

"I must be the father!"

All adult eyes focused on Al.

"Are you out of your fucking mind?" she declared, forcing herself to talk slowly, to avoid having the words reflect the tornado in her skull.

She was able to shove him now, hard, towards the door. She felt grateful, or disappointed? that she did not have a hammer in her hand because she would've slammed his face with it.

But Wynn barely budged.

"I got the sperm from a cryobank," offered Al, as she looked at Maddie's shocked expression. "Unless you jerked off for money and we got your sperm by chance you're being delusional. Let's go. Now!"

He continued to resist her efforts to move him and said, "I never jerked off for money, but I did fuck in this room."

Maddie latched onto the side of the changing table to settle herself.

"So what?" responded Al, trying desperately to keep calm. "Just because we fucked once doesn't mean your sperm ended up in Maddie. That's not possible.

Now are you walking out with me, or do you want to get carried out on a stretcher?"

Her grip was so tight it had to hurt, but Wynn seemed oblivious.

"I wouldn't think it possible either," he said. "And I wouldn't have thought anything of it. Except…"

He jerked his arm free of Al's grasp and used his left hand to lift up his dirty tee shirt while his right hand pointed towards the distinct protrusion of a left rib.

"A family trait."

Al and Maddie stared at the rib, transfixed, then simultaneously looked over at Jesse, still in just a diaper, and saw the identical left rib protrusion, only in miniature.

"I don't think I'm leaving just yet," said Wynn with a huge smile. "I think we should all sit down and have breakfast together. Like one big happy family."

CHAPTER TWENTY-THREE

As Wynn devoured breakfast with animal need, raspberry jam smeared across his scruffy beard, Al and Maddie just stared at him.

He ate as if the weight of the world had been lifted off his shoulders.

Al wished she had smothered his face with the pillow for just a little longer.

She wondered when his negotiations would begin.

Perhaps from the fullness of his first hearty meal in a while, or from the prospect of having a safe comfortable place to rest, Wynn went right from the breakfast table to the couch and nodded out once again.

Al had already called in sick at work. They took Jesse for a stroll in the carriage.

At the park, they sat on a lone bench away from the playground area where the group of mothers sat. Maddie waved. They waved back. Al seemed lost in her own thoughts. Maddie could see the moms whispering discreetly while they looked over, but she was happy they finally got to see her with Al.

"Tell me what's going on," said Maddie.

"My first year in college Wynn put himself on the line and saved me from frat boys jerking off on me as part of their initiation."

"What?"

"No matter how fucked up Wynn is, he proved he's not a rapist."

"You didn't tell him what it was for?"

"I rented a porno and just wanted him to jerk off into a condom. But he couldn't get it up. So I—"

"Oh, Al."

"I married Wynn, let him stay with me numerous times, kept him afloat. He saved us money we didn't have and donated some sperm. We don't owe him anything."

"He's Jesse's biological father. We owe him something."

Though Maddie didn't like that she had been lied to, she was still blown away by the full extent of the sacrifice Al had made. Maddie filled with deep tenderness towards her partner. If she thought Al would allow it, she would have pulled Al close, embraced her, comforted her, mothers or no mothers watching.

"He won't want custody," said Al. "Hates responsibility. Sees this as a permanent ride on our gravy train. Roof over his head. Food. Chance to remain the only person he knows how to be: a lazy, stoned, piece of shit."

"Can we afford it?"

"Look at me." Maddie's eyes immediately riveted on her partner. "There's no fucking way Wynn's ever going to touch Jesse, let alone be in his life. He's a parasite, a user, an alcoholic, an addict, and a scumbag. This is about giving Jesse the chances we never had. Wynn's way more than a bump in that road."

"I understand."

"Nod your head like you understand."

Maddie nodded.

"Now say to me: 'I promise not to let Wynn touch Jesse nor feel any sympathy for an asshole like Wynn.'"

"I promise not to let Wynn touch Jess nor feel any sympathy for...Wynn."

"We promise him a roof over his head and a monthly allowance. We don't put it in writing. In return, he signs over all custody and we push through my official adoption as soon as possible."

"Won't he cause trouble if we don't live up to our end?"

"Jesse has given us a new life but we also need a fresh start. Away from your mother, away from Lancer and fucked up Fox, and all the pre-conceived notions this town has about the dyke couple and the baby."

Al looked over at the moms staring at them. She moved closer to Maddie on the bench. The moms began whispering again.

"Let's begin a whole new life far away from here," she continued, "maybe in a densely populated area, maybe the east coast, maybe with different names, so no one can find us, especially Wynn."

"I know I don't see Mother anymore," said Maddie, a quiver in her voice, "but it's a comfort knowing she's nearby and I'm nearby. What if something happened to her?"

"You can be in phone contact with her nurse."

"I can't be three thousand miles away."

"Just imagine there's a giant leech attached to your body, my body, Jesse's body. No one can see it, but each day it sucks some life out of us. That's what your mother did to you. That's what my father did to me. That's what Wynn will do to us."

Maddie had to stand. She undid the brake on Jesse's carriage. Walked west. Al next to her.

"I really don't want to leave Mother and I really don't want to be looking over my shoulder, worried someone's going to take our baby away. Let's see what Wynn has to say. He seems like a simple soul. There's got to be a way to work this out so he's satisfied, it's all legal, and we get back on track with the life Jesse, you, and I deserve."

"Yes, what you, I, and Jesse deserve."

They walked as long as they could, enjoying this time together that usually only happened on odd weekends. But then the clouds darkened and they hurried home, just barely inside before being drenched by the arriving storm.

"Great news!" Wynn declared from the couch, long legs extended onto the coffee table, shoes still on, huge smile pasted across his face.

Al was already queasy.

224

"I called my father at work."

She ran to the kitchen. Dry retched over the sink. Maddie picked up Jesse. Held him close.

"He's in Japan on business. As usual his secretary wouldn't connect me. But when I explained I wanted to talk about his *grandson* he called me back right away."

Maddie had to sit in a chair.

"He was overjoyed. Both my sisters have girls and there are no boys to carry on the family name."

Al stumbled back in, collapsed on another chair in the living room.

"Cheer up. He's not so bad. I'm the one who fucked up. He's loaded. He'll totally dote on the kid. Do you know how much college costs these days? Jesse will have everything he wants."

"What does your father want?" asked Al.

"Desperately wants a grandson, a baller to carry on the family name. With your DNA and mine the kid will be a world class athlete."

"He doesn't have my DNA, dipshit."

Wynn looked at Maddie. "Well I know you're both good people and he'll be a great kid."

Wynn stared at their stunned faces.

"Don't you understand? We'll all be set up. I've been on his shitlist for so long and this is finally a chance to make it right. I bet he gives me a big salary with his company."

Al couldn't take it anymore. She stood, jumped directly towards Wynn, grabbed a fistful of his tee shirt with each hand, jerked him to his feet, her faces inches from his chest as he cowered and she spit, "Answer my question, motherfucker! What does he want?"

Maddie was too afraid to ask Al to calm down. Jesse began to whimper. Maddie swayed him in her arms.

Al let go of Wynn's shirt and took a step back.

Wynn let out a grateful sigh, knowing he had been very close to being clocked.

He said, meekly, "I think he wants to bring us to Canada."

Maddie's swaying arms froze. Both of Al's fists clenched as she stepped back into Wynn's face.

"Who's *us*?"

Wynn dropped back onto the couch.

"Me, uh, Jesse," he stuttered. "And yeah, I'm sure Maddie, she's the mom. And you, Al, you're my bud."

Al's brain clouded so strongly that the only thing she was sure of was that at this point Wynn's demise wouldn't help.

"Hey, relax. My dad's cutting short his Japan trip and I'm sure he'll explain everything when he comes down at the end of the week to see his grandson."

That night, while Wynn snored on the couch, Al and Maddie lay in their respective beds, unable to sleep.

Al tossed and turned, tore at her bedding, battled with her demon pillow and sheets as she had done the night she had heard her father was dying and wanted to see her. Her heart hammered with rage while her mind pinballed the prospect of their vision being annihilated.

And again, Maddie could only stare with helplessness, wondering what she could do to help her partner.

"Wynn's father, Whit, doted on Wynn every step of the way," rattled Al as she wrestled on the bed. "Until Wynn fucked up with the accident then it was *sayonara*. He's a dominant patriarch who only cares about himself. Stealing Wynn's sperm, impregnating you without his knowledge could provide a pretty good case for shared custody. Who knows what a sonofabitch with money can do, maybe even *lose* custody? Access to the best lawyers, ones we couldn't afford. We're unmarried, presumed by all to be a lesbian couple, I have a psychiatric and criminal history. Whit's probably exactly like my old man."

Al punched her pillow several times, then threw all of the bedding onto the floor, including the fitted sheet. She curled into a fetal position, lying in a pool of sweat, exhausted, beaten, barely enough strength to whisper.

"I'm so sorry, Maddie. I just wanted what's best for us. I never thought it would come to this."

When the first rays of dawn streamed through the one window, Maddie saw Al was still in the same position, curled more helplessly than Jesse.

Maddie got out of bed, dropped to her knees by Al's mattress, swelling with great compassion for the partner she loved. Despite Maddie's voice remaining at a deliberate low pitch, it transmitted all of the ferocity of a mother lion protecting her cub.

"Let's get the hell out of Oregon."

CHAPTER TWENTY-FOUR

The next day, Al went to work as usual. They would wait until the end of the week to bolt, just before Whit was scheduled to arrive, so they could cash their last paychecks and close out their bank accounts. They would leave most of their belongings behind. They didn't have much and they didn't want Wynn to get suspicious.

Maddie had expressed concern about departing Lancer without giving notice, but Al had explained that this was the best time to do it, as she was still on maternity leave and a replacement was already working.

Al didn't give a rat fuck about leaving Lancer unannounced. She hated the place. She hated Fox Phelps. She was full of manic joy from the impending journey all three of them were about to embark on, one that would take them far away from all that held them down.

Fuck the Seroquel as well.

She needed maximum energy to carry out the final tasks germane to their departure.

Al busied herself emptying all of the trash cans in the gym then headed up to the athletic department offices. She liked that she was nearly invisible. Who wanted to acknowledge that the former softball coach was now the trash lady anyway?

She worked with briskness and efficiency, dumping small baskets of trash into the large, wheeled barrel she had brought with her. Most of the athletic staff worked with their office doors open and Al noticed Fox typing at his computer. She completed her tasks, took the trash barrel into the elevator, headed back down to the gym floor.

Not long after, the fire alarm went off. There was no smell of smoke and no one had been informed of any drills and some would like to have stayed to finish their work, but the alarm was so loud, so annoying that this was not possible and everyone immediately left the building.

Except Al.

She was hidden in a stall in the women's bathroom, a plug in each ear. When she was sure everyone must be gone, she crept quietly back up the stairs. She had on a pair of latex gloves she had swiped from Maddie's athletic training kit.

She entered Fox's office and was delighted that he was still logged on, in the middle of drafting an email. She pulled a piece of paper from her back pocket which had a list of websites. With the same briskness and efficiency she had used to empty the trash, she began to type in the various web addresses, logging on, browsing, randomly visiting pages, then moving onto the next one.

There were many times these last months since Fox had stolen her job and had executed his plan for humiliating her that she had dwelled on *her* plan, hatched it, fine-tuned it.

Al finished up, logged off the websites, left the computer on with the open email Fox had been composing. She made sure everything was in the same place as when she had sat down. She took off the latex gloves, the only thing that had touched the computer keys, and made her way down the back stairs of the building, then exited through a secluded emergency door.

Maddie's final visit with Mother couldn't have worked out any better, though Maddie didn't want to consider this her *final* visit. There would be time away, but she believed that she would be back, whenever she could, to look in on Mother. She told the floor supervisor that she would be gone for a while and got his cell number so she could check up on Mother from time to time. What was perfect about this morning's visit was that Jesse was asleep in the car with Al, and Mother was alone and asleep when Maddie came into her room.

She pulled up a chair beside the bed. She spoke aloud, but so quietly it couldn't possibly wake her.

"I wish this could be different, that you could be in our lives as a loving grandmother to Jesse, as a mother who respected me and my partner. I wish Jesse's grandfather was someone who could understand how important it is for Jesse to be with his *two* parents, but I'm pretty sure he's not. So we have to do this. I'm not forsaking you, but I'll be embracing a new life, one that's ours and no one else's. One that continues to give us the freedom to shape our lives in a way that's rewarding and fruitful. Hopefully you'll see someday what a beautiful, brilliant, happy boy Jesse will be. No one on this earth will be loved more. Hopefully one day you accept him. That would complete my life in the fullest way possible. Know that I love you, care for you, always tried my best. But now it's time to start over."

Maddie found a pen and a piece of paper. She wrote on it that she loved Mother and that she would always be with her in some way. She folded it and left it on the night table.

She stood. Mother was on her side, uncovered, in her nightgown. This really was the best part about Mother being lost in the throes of her last dose of medication. Maddie got into the bed and aligned her body against the zig-zag of Mother's bent waist and knees, spooned herself tight against Mother's fragile frame as she had done so often as a little girl when Mother was out like this. They were the same height now and their bodies meshed perfectly, but Maddie crunched up to make herself as small as possible. She hugged, but not too tight, not wanting to awaken Mother and ruin this perfect moment by seeing her recoil, hearing her say something nasty. She inhaled the unique scent of Mother's hair, squeezed one more time, then finally let go.

Maddie stood, leaned over the bed. Mother's face was without makeup, and presented a view Maddie had rarely seen during the last few years: the dark half-moons of flesh under the eyes, the heavy creases in her face, the baggy flaps of skin resting heavily around her throat, wispy unplucked hairs sprouting from her ears. Mother had aged fast since living full time in the Senior Center. Maddie wished that somehow all four of them could've lived together, that Mother could come with them now. But it was not meant to be. Maddie leaned down and kissed Mother on the cheek. Her sleeping body remained perfectly still. Maddie exited the room. Mother's eyes popped open.

In the parking lot, Maddie opened the Honda's passenger door, relieved to see that Jesse was still sound asleep.

Our angel, she thought.

Al searched her face for signs of how the farewell went and Maddie smiled back and said, "I'm as ready as I'll ever be."

Each night they packed a little so as not to arouse Wynn's suspicions, and stored their suitcases and bags in the bedroom closet. Al mapped out a trip across the northern route of the U.S., regaling Maddie with stories of New York City, a place she had visited twice during national softball tournaments.

"There are so many fucking people in the streets that no one notices if it's two women together, two women and a baby, two women who dress alike, one with a screwed up haircut, the other prematurely gray. No one gives a shit. They just leave you be."

"Sounds wonderful," said Maddie, excited about this adventure, but concerned about Al's giddy energy that had been non-stop ever since Maddie had given the green light.

The next day, while Al was at work, Maddie signed for a FedEx package that was delivered to their apartment and addressed to Al. She placed it on Al's bed, left it unopened, but remained intensely curious.

Al came home. Maddie had prepared dinner for all of them, but Al took her food to the bedroom. Wynn ate in silence. He basically slept and ate all day. His happiness from his father's upcoming visit dwindled into anxiousness. He washed his one set of clothes every evening. He had left the house only once and that was for a shave and a haircut, paid for by money Maddie had given him.

When Maddie finished cleaning up after dinner, she retired to the bedroom. Al reclined on the bed, eyes wide open. The package was gone.

"What'was in the FedEx?" asked Maddie.

"Nothing."

"As I've said all along, if this is going to work we have to trust each other."

"A safety net."

Maddie placed Jesse in the bassinet, sat on her bed, looked at Al, waited for more.

"There would be no point in going on without you and Jesse," said Al. "Life would be too painful."

"I can't imagine anything that could break us up completely."

"A lot of mean things happen when you end up in the world of the *caught*."

"What do you mean?"

"Some live in this world, do bad things, and get to live their lives the way they want, the *uncaught*."

"Like Fox?"

"Then there are those who are *caught*, who pay the price, like when I went to Juvie, slapped Fox, my dad when they discovered his planted pedo stash."

"Planted?"

"It's essential that you, Jesse, and I remain *uncaught*. Which means whatever it takes to keep Jesse away from a megalomaniac grandfather and a loser father who could never love him the way we do."

"Have you been taking the Seroquel?"

"If I somehow can't protect you I couldn't bear it and wouldn't want to go on."

"Dr. Drummond?"

"Who?"

"What's in the package?"

"Potassium chloride, sodium thiopental, and three syringes."

"Oh, lord," escaped Maddie's lips, then all of the air seemed to disappear from the room and she had trouble breathing.

"From a pharmaceutical black market. One's lethal, the other an anesthetic to relieve any discomfort."

Maddie reached her hands up to her eyes.

Al stood, looked down on her, so close they were almost touching.

"I promise not to do anything you don't agree to. I fully expect to live the life we dreamt. This guarantees it. We can't risk losing Jesse and exposing him to meanness. If we're all together, everything's perfect, whether in this world or the next."

Maddie trembled all over.

Al dropped to her knees so she could now look up, mesmerizing Maddie with her deep stare.

"Do you trust me?" asked Al.

"Yes."

"Do you trust that I'd never hurt you or Jesse?"

"Yes."

"Then put your faith in me. Trust that I've thought this through and come up with an option that binds us together no matter what happens."

Al was so close, Maddie thought Al might kiss her.

"You made this all happen, Al. You had a vision and that vision's been realized. I want us to be together...forever."

"You've shown me, Maddie, that without trust there can't be love. I'll always cherish this love we've created...together."

Two days later—before the morning Whit Davis was supposed to arrive from Canada—in the dark of night, car loaded, as Wynn snored loudly on the couch—Al, Maddie, and Jesse left McCannville and headed east.

Once on the highway, Al turned the radio up loud, but was able to yell above the music.

"We fuckin' did it!"

Maddie turned to the backseat, grabbed Jesse's hand, rocked it to the melody.

Maddie shouted even louder.

"No one can stop us now!"

CHAPTER TWENTY-FIVE

Freedom!

No jobs. Driving in the dark, out on the open road, just days ahead where they could spend all of their time as a family.

"I've wanted to get out of McCannville my whole life," said Maddie. "No one will ever call me a germatoid or dork again, no fat kid will humiliate me, the biggest loser in the state won't reject me, no dirty looks from moms I thought were my friends."

"No smirks because the softball coach is the janitor," added Al. "No pompous boss who thinks he can control me, no drunken leech attached to my side, no asshole grandfather who thinks he can step in and steal our life to fulfill his."

Jesse burped in the backseat.

"Our son!" they chimed together.

Al turned up the radio and she and Maddie sang along as they belted out hit after hit from their high school days.

Moving east, away, in closed quarters together, made the car seem to be the safest place in the world.

They drove over the border into Idaho just as the sun came up. They stopped for food, a bathroom break, gas.

Maddie took Jesse into the convenience store for a quick change. Al told Maddie to pick up a box of donuts and plenty of chocolate bars.

While Al waited in the car for the gas attendant, her mind and body wound down from the rush of their escape. A weary contentment washed over her. Wynn would have no idea where they went and was probably still comatose on the couch.

"Did you get gas?" Maddie asked when she returned with Jesse and their provisions.

Al opened her eyes, realized she had nodded off. She looked again for an attendant then noticed several people pumping their own gas.

"Oh, shit. I forgot that Oregon's like the only state with full serve."

She got out of the car, pre-paid inside with cash. They had cut up their credit cards the day before leaving McCannville.

After driving another six hours, they found themselves on the outskirts of Salt Lake City. Maddie insisted they see the lake. They parked, got out, and took in the vast liquid greenness of this unique body of water. Adults walked along the shores, some with kids.

"Look at this beautiful lake, Jesse," said Maddie. "One day soon we'll teach you how to swim."

Jesse fumbled at Maddie's jacket.

"Hungry again?" asked Maddie. "Where do you put it all?"

"Great athletes need their fuel," said Al with an exhausted smile.

"I think I'm tapped out."

Al pulled a pre-mixed bottle out of the diaper bag and handed it to her partner.

They sat on a bench. Maddie stared at the lake, fed Jesse.

"I've only been in two other states aside from Oregon," she said. "And that was mostly softball fields and motel rooms."

Al stared at Jesse sucking on the bottle.

"We're a family in Oregon, Idaho, now Utah," she said. "Then all of the other eight states we'll pass through before we get to New York City. A *family* no matter where we go."

When Maddie was done with the feeding, they got back into the car, found a local motel, paid in cash once more, and Al immediately fell asleep on her twin bed.

Darkness had fully settled in when Al opened her eyes again, wide awake, already buzzed. Jesse was asleep on a blanket in the bottom drawer that was pulled out from the one dresser. Al looked at the digital clock: 10:42pm. Maddie wasn't moving in her bed. Al tossed and turned, went outside for a walk, would've welcomed some pot to smooth the edges, had packed Seroquel but needed all of her energy for this arduous journey. She went back in, couldn't sit still.

"Maddie, Maddie…"

Maddie turned on her side, faced Al, asked sleepily, "You okay?"

"Ready to get back on the road."

"No reason to rush. Let's enjoy the trip. So much to see during the daylight."

"I'm getting antsy."

"Try to relax."

Al flopped on top of the comforter.

"Maddie, if you had the opportunity to have any man in the world make love to you, who would it be?"

"Why do you ask?"

"I want you to be happy."

"You make me happy."

"I want to know who would make you happy that way."

"Brad Pitt."

"His hair's always so greasy."

"He's very sexy and loves kids."

"Close your eyes."

"Okay."

"Imagine Brad Pitt climbs into bed with you. Imagine his hard body, that six pack he had in that movie. What was it? Saw it as a kid."

"*Thelma and Louise.*"

"He was skinnier then."

"But so hot!"

"Imagine him naked with you. You're naked. He wraps his arms around you."

"Mmm..."

"I want you to have everything. Even the things I can't give. Do you feel how hard you're making him, how he can't wait to be inside you?"

"Al."

"Yes."

"Brad Pitt is really sexy and I can't tell you how many times I fantasized about him while growing up, but I don't need him to make me happy. Didn't he steal their money in the morning?" Maddie laughed. "He can't be trusted. I trust you."

"Are you happy now?"

"As happy as I've ever been. The only day that was better was the day Jesse was born and the day we all hugged in the parking lot."

"Sorry I've been out of sorts since then."

"Once we're in New York everything will be perfect again."

"Do you want me to talk to you like I usually do, as if it's me touching you?"

"That would be lovely."

"Do you want me to have a penis this time?"

"I don't need a penis to make me happy."

Those words warmed Al even more, and she took her time, used descriptions as vivid and as creative as she could think of and made aural love to Maddie that climaxed with her partner's deep moans of pleasure.

When they were done, there was a brief silence as Maddie caught her breath.

"I don't know if I can ever physically do all I just said," whispered Al. "But I hope one day we can sleep in the same bed. I hope one day that I can at least kiss you and hold you."

"That would be unbelievable," sighed Maddie. "For now we can be grateful for how far we've come and how fortunate we are to have found the other, and, most of all, how fantastic it is to be the parents of little Jesse."

They closed their eyes and fell into the most blissful slumber either could remember.

In the morning, Al got up to shower first. Maddie turned on the TV. The morning news came on. She sat on the bed. The female newscaster said, "We broke the news yesterday about the gay porn scandal that's rocked McCannville, Oregon and has tongues wagging all over the state."

"Oh my God!" exclaimed Maddie.

Al came out of the bathroom, fully dressed, hair still wet, eyes immediately riveted on the TV.

"Well today it's been announced that Lancer College athletic director Fox Phelps has been suspended without pay, pending further investigation, for allegedly visiting gay porn sites on his office computer, which included *Hairy Bears*, *Smiling Twinks*, and *Bondage Daddies*. He currently remains cloistered in his home to escape the fervent public outcry and has issued a statement that all charges are false. Nevertheless, he has been ex-communicated from his church where he served as a deacon for over twenty years."

Maddie looked suspiciously at Al, who couldn't stop grinning.

"*My* end-of-the-year evaluation for Fox Phelps: Welcome to the world of the *caught*."

"The situation in McCannville has turned even more salacious," continued the newscaster, "with public accusations that two women, from the very same Lancer athletic department, stole a man's sperm without his knowledge, conceived a child, and after being discovered have vanished completely. On site at the local courthouse, Eugene Marks has both the alleged father and grandfather of the baby. Wynn and Whit Davis."

Maddie grabbed Jesse out of the drawer.

"Tell me I'm fucking dreaming," said Al.

Wynn and Whit stood next to Eugene, who held the microphone up to Whit, who was broad shouldered, decked out in a crisp blue suit. He reminded Al of Wynn in college, before all the drugs and drinking had taken its toll, only Whit had a fuller face and a thick bush of white hair. In the background was a statue of General McCann.

"I've alerted the proper authorities," said Whit. "Hired a top notch private investigator to track these two down, and the number one PR firm in the U.S. to get the word out across the country to help us corral this devious couple. My son's seed was stolen against his will! I'm sorry if I'm being politically incorrect here, but I will use all resources at my disposal to make sure that no *grandson* of mine is raised by lesbian fugitives."

Whit threw his arm around Wynn who was clean-shaven, also wearing a suit and tie, and had on the most obnoxious, shit-eating grin Al had ever seen.

The vision that under both their shirts was the same left rib protrusion that Jesse had made Al sick to her stomach.

Maddie held Jesse tighter.

Al calmly grabbed the TV remote, smashed it against the wall, instantly silencing the newscast, inspiring a nervous yelp in the baby.

"No more sightseeing. No more sleeping. We're getting to New York as fast as we can."

In the parking lot of the Salt Lake City motel, Maddie waited in the car with Jesse, while Al, with a Swiss Army knife, quickly unscrewed the front and back license plates from the Toyota parked next to them. Al tossed the plates onto the back seat of the Honda, got in, then sped towards the highway.

"That's illegal," said Maddie.

"Least of our problems."

At the first empty rest stop, Al put the Utah plates on the Honda and tossed the Oregon ones into the bushes.

She stopped in the next town and bought each of them big sunglasses and Maddie a large floppy sun hat, and for herself a two-toned trucker's cap.

"We'll soon be home free," said Al.

"I'm scared."

"Everything's under my control."

Al drove like a madwoman through Utah and Wyoming: She was well over the speed limit, but careful not to be the fastest on the road, not to stay too long in the left lane, to keep her eyes peeled for radar traps, to slow down before inclines when she couldn't see what was on the other side.

Her voice raced like the car when she made up rules for the trip:

"We wear our disguises at all times, in public I'm Bea, you're Sylvia, Jesse's Hank, no more eating in restaurants or rest stops, we never go inside somewhere together, either alone, or it's just Sylvia and Hank, no more watching TV or listening to the radio."

It was nighttime when they made it to Nebraska and Maddie finally harnessed the courage to say, "You need to take the Seroquel again."

"What makes you think I'm not?"

Maddie didn't answer.

Eyes glued to the road, face twitchy, mind wired from all of the sugar and non-stop driving, Al sneered, "Don't tell me what to do."

Maddie stared out the window.

"I'm sorry," said Al after they had passed another dozen or so cornfields. "I need to stay focused and keep up my energy. Once we're in New York I'll be the woman you fell in love with, the relaxed parent Jesse needs."

Somewhere around Des Moines, Iowa, fifteen hours from Salt Lake City, it wasn't the car, but Al who ran out of gas.

It was as if the TV newscast had been steadily pumping oxygen into her as she relentlessly pounded the highway, until her bubble finally burst and everything fizzled into a shriveled mess.

She closed her eyes, bobbed her head, the Honda swerved, Maddie yelled, "Al!" as she grabbed the wheel to steady the car, which caused Al's head to jerk, her eyes to snap open, and her mouth to bark, "Leave it!"

Maddie immediately took her hands off the wheel.

Al realized she needed to pull over immediately to the side of the road to sleep for a few hours. But that might attract more attention and Jesse would get cold. And with the way the fatigue had abruptly bombarded her body, she probably needed more than a few hours.

At this moment, she wished that she had had more patience when it came to teaching Maddie to drive.

Al checked them into the only motel around, a real dump, while Maddie and Jesse waited in the car. Then she drove around to their room and they got out. Al passed out on the bed. Maddie breastfed Jesse and got him settled. She was tempted to turn on the TV to see if there were any further developments, to see if they were in any kind of danger or on some law enforcement Most Wanted list, but she did not want to risk the wrath of Al.

She also wanted to find out more about Fox Phelps. Even if he was cleared, he would always have the stigma in a town the size of McCannville.

Later, Al opened her eyes in a foggy haze and saw that the covers to Maddie's bed had been pulled back and that Jesse was asleep next to Maddie on the bed.

"Put him in the dresser drawer," mumbled Al. "I don't want you to fall asleep and turn over and smother him."

Maddie didn't want to get into a discussion about how gross this place was and that the dresser drawers were disgusting, so she simply said, "Okay."

Al drifted back to sleep.

In the morning, Maddie was already up and showered and breastfeeding when Al finally stirred. Al looked at the light beaming through the translucent window shades and said, "Shit, Maddie, why did you let me sleep so late?"

"You need your rest."

They put on their hats and sunglasses before exiting the motel room and hitting the road. They stopped for an Egg McMuffin for Maddie. Al was content with donuts and chocolate. She continued to drive hard. The car would've been completely silent if not for Jesse's fussing.

As tiny and undeveloped as he was, he seemed to have a sophisticated radar for the mood of his parents. It was as if he did not want to be in the car seat. At one point, Maddie went into the back with him, tried to soothe him with steady, nurturing verbal patter, while feeding him as often as she could. When being fed or held, Jesse was at peace. Maddie wanted to keep holding him even after he had his fill of milk, the fear of somehow losing him making it hard to give up these tender moments. But Al would insist she put him back, that he was safer strapped in. Until a little while later he would fuss again and then Maddie had to set him free.

Just outside of Chicago, about five hours into that day's drive, they needed gas and provisions.

Maddie and Jesse went into the convenience store first, used the bathroom. Al went in to pre-pay the gas, then returned to the car to fill up. She waited as long as she could for Maddie and Jesse to come out, shifting nervously from one foot to the other, but finally had to go in to pee. Just before ducking into the ladies' room, Al saw Maddie, with Jesse tucked against her chest, looking at a display, seemingly unsure about what brand of beef jerky to buy.

Maddie wanted to prolong this stop as much as possible. It was like extracting teeth to get Al to pull over. Jesse was getting claustrophobic in the car. They all needed fresher air.

There was just one worker behind the counter and not much patronage at this time of day. Over and behind his head a TV was tuned to a tabloid news magazine. Maddie had been ignoring the sound, which was turned low. She was immediately startled when her eyes raised to the TV screen and she saw her photo and Al's photo, their pics from the Lancer athletic website.

She was grateful for their disguises. Maddie knew she should take Jesse to the car, but instead pretended to look at magazines as she inched closer to hear what the male and female moderators, sitting on tall chairs in a studio, were saying.

"The whereabouts of the Lancer College fugitive moms remains a mystery," the woman reported. "While the latest development has the biological grandmother coming forward to affirm that her daughter has definitely produced a virgin birth, prompting some fringe religious groups to label this the Second Coming, or a possible prelude to the Rapture."

The cashier, clearly annoyed, reached for the remote to change the channel. One channel also had their pics, along with Fox's. Another had clips of the Lancer campus. He stopped at a newscast for a second, only to realize the report was about the same story. And to Maddie's further horror and embarrassment she saw Mother being interviewed in the rec room of the Senior Center, her hair completely done up and set, full makeup on, wearing her best church dress, smiling, nodding, clearly enjoying all of the attention. The channel stayed on long enough for Maddie to hear Mother say, "It's an immaculate miracle. No other way to explain it."

Just as Al came out of the bathroom, the cashier let out an exasperated sigh, put the remote down, leaving the TV on the original tabloid show channel Maddie had first seen.

"The biological grandfather," said the male moderator, "also continues to attract nationwide media attention with his sordid tale of stolen sperm and his one man crusade to find *Mother Maddie*, as she is now being called by some, and her partner, and of course baby Jesse."

Hearing the nickname, their son's name on TV, caused both mothers to wince with discomfort. Al moved quickly towards the cash register.

"Authorities have released information that the car they are driving may be a Honda CR-V with Oregon plates. Though there may be a link to some stolen plates in a Utah motel parking lot. They ask anyone with information to please contact your local police."

It was unclear whether the cashier was listening or not. Al wanted to get the fuck out of the store and back on the road, but she needed to move Maddie along, who remained transfixed by what was happening on the TV.

Al picked up six candy bars and threw them on the checkout counter.

"It's amazing how so many throughout the country have been captivated by this intense story, as well as by the morals scandal involving the boss of these two women that has outraged the small town of McCannville and polarized most of the state. Sarah, what's the word on the streets of Portland?"

Al saw the security cameras in the store. She was sure there were others out by the gas pumps, the Utah plates clearly visible. She hastily pulled out a twenty dollar bill and slammed it over the candy bars, immediately capturing the cashier's attention. While he concentrated on ringing her up, Al tried to catch Maddie's eye and motion her towards the car with her head.

"It has been quite a couple of days here in the Pacific Northwest," said Sarah on the TV. A man with short brown hair stood next to her. Behind her was a large crowd. "Next to me is Mr. Tom Lasker, head of the local Portland LGBTQ Alliance. Mr. Lasker, can you share your thoughts about what's happening?"

"I certainly had no idea McCannville was such a steamy hotbed," he said with a coy smile. "As far as Fox Phelps, you are welcome to come to Portland anytime. We'll make you feel a lot more at home. As far as the two moms." Lasker turned now and looked into the camera, as if staring directly at them, and raised his voice to an animated pitch. "You go, girls! Wherever you are we all hope you make it!"

The crowd let out a raucous cheer.

The cashier placed Al's change on her candy bars. He had a pencil thin black moustache. He looked up at the TV and said, "I hate dykes."

"What did you just say?"

The cashier turned back to her, clearly off automatic pilot now, and finally took notice of his customer. "Oh, sorry."

Al couldn't help reaching into her pocket to grip the Swiss Army knife.

Maddie approached with Jesse.

"Bea, it's time to go. Hank's getting fussy."

The cashier was surprised to hear Maddie speak and seemed even more surprised that the three of them were together. He looked at Maddie and the baby, then back at Al. Al was desperately trying to figure out if he had made their identities. At the very least the cashier caught the menace in Al's expression and tried to smooth things over with, "Very cute baby. Very cute."

"It's time for you to shut the fuck up!"

Al didn't like him even looking at Jesse, let alone commenting on him.

The cashier took a step back, his nervousness causing him to chatter in a clipped, rapid tempo: "I don't want trouble. I don't know what's with this country. So damn impolite. Just talking. Expressing my opinion. Don't forget free speech!"

Al took the knife out of her pocket, opened it.

"I respect freedom. I respect mothers. I love babies!"

Maddie stepped closer and reached out a free hand towards Al's arm to nudge her towards the door.

"But they need fathers, too!"

"Don't ever talk about my baby!" screamed Al as she lunged over the counter towards the cashier.

Maddie's touch misdirected the blade and it only sliced across the fleshy softness of his shoulder, instantly drawing blood.

The cashier was totally stunned, needing a moment to realize he was cut. By that time the moms had fled towards the Honda, Jesse wrapped tight in Maddie's arms, and were soon peeling out of the lot and back on the road.

No one said anything. Maddie, still in the back, strapped Jesse into his car seat. Al tore off the hat and sunglasses.

"You do the same!" she snapped.

Maddie obliged.

Al made it to downtown Chicago. She pulled into an underground parking lot, found a secluded spot. She shut the car engine and all three remained quiet and motionless in the dank darkness of the building.

"I'm sorry," Al finally offered. "I'll get a grip. Promise. I just didn't like what he was saying."

"The more illegal stuff you do the worse it will be for all of us."

Al turned back to her, face weary with emotion.

"I've tried so hard, but like everything I touch, it turns to shit."

"You're not shit. I'm not shit. Jesse's not shit," said Maddie firmly, surprising Al with the profanity. "We're all beautiful. You must believe that. Otherwise we're doomed."

Al closed her eyes, tried to rest. So did Maddie. Jesse was already sleeping. Al's plan was to wait until nighttime, then drive the 800 miles straight to New York where they would sell the car as soon as possible, buy some black market identity papers, get a significant makeover, and set up house, maybe even marry.

They were so close.

IMMACULATE CONCEPTION

After sunset, before Al steered the Honda out of the Chicago underground parking lot, she discreetly procured a set of New Mexico license plates from a car on the same floor.

Al doubled her fury. If she had an airplane-sized fuel tank she would not have stopped at all.

"New rules," she barked, once on the highway, jerking Maddie awake. "I pee, buy supplies as needed, gas up. You and Jesse wait in the car. Your bathroom breaks are at restaurants and supermarkets. Never all three at once. Less chance of being near a TV."

She bit into a candy bar, gorged on sugar donuts—white powder spread across her cheeks—washed it all down with swigs of apple juice.

As they motored through each new state—Indiana, Ohio, finally Pennsylvania—putting more distance between them and Chicago—their heavy moods steadily lightened.

"Must have played a softball tournament in every corner of this state," declared Al. "Who wants to see Mommy hit a home run?"

Jesse gurgled from the backseat.

Maddie smiled.

Al floored the Honda, fought off fatigue anyway she could.

"I promise to take my meds again once we get settled. Jesse, you're a real trooper, just keep sitting tight. Maddie, you want to drive, hah, hah?"

Maddie had to laugh.

"I'll teach in you in New York. Really. If you can drive there, you can drive anywhere."

"I would like that."

More donuts, chocolate, juice.

Al opened the window for a blast of cold air.

"Jesse," said Maddie.

Al closed the window.

"Sorry."

"Let's stop at the next rest area."

"No way."

Al rubbed her calf.

"Your leg cramping again?" asked Maddie.

"Old MacDonald had a farm, E-I, E-I, O."

Big road sign: *WELCOME TO NEW JERSEY!*

"Woowee!" belted Maddie, knowing they were into their last lap. She looked up from Al's smartphone. "Once we get to the end of New Jersey we leave Route 80, head south on the New Jersey Turnpike, then east on 495 through the Lincoln Tunnel and straight into Manhattan."

The landscape had changed from the tree-lined hills of Pennsylvania to the city lights of the more densely populated New Jersey.

Al reached for one more donut, but couldn't bear to take another bite and tossed it out the window.

"We should stop," said Maddie. "We're so close, a little break won't mean much."

"No, no, no, no. We'll soon have plenty of time to sleep."

But Al's head bobbed once more. Maddie didn't want to go through having to grab the wheel again. She just kept talking, loudly, with much animation.

"We'll get a really nice apartment. I can take in kids to babysit while you coach softball, or maybe it's better for you to do something different so no one recognizes you. We can keep Bea, Sylvia, and Hank if you want. But Jesse will always be Jesse with us. No burdens at all. No Fox, Wynn, Whit. I'll miss Mother but I'll check up on her. I'll call the nurse from a payphone. Al, we're so very close. You crossed so much of the country in so little time. You have such prodigious strength, superhuman conviction, infinite fortitude, epic focus and concentration. I know we'll realize our dream. But we must get there *safely*."

Once on the New Jersey Turnpike, the lights of the New York City skyline visible to the east, Al's monster sugar rush plummeted down and she landed with the most intense crash of exhaustion yet.

Her eyes went glassy, the highway seemed to shimmer, her neck felt rubbery as fatigue swallowed her whole. It might have been a true disaster, if the yellow gas warning light hadn't begun to flash wildly.

"Al!"

"Motherfucker!" shouted Al, startling Jesse, as she slapped an open palm, hard, against the steering wheel. "We can make it. Once we're in New York I'll just park this shit somewhere, we'll walk, take a subway, leave it all behind."

"Let's find a gas station now, take just a little break," pleaded Maddie. "The traffic's getting worse. It must be rush hour. We can't afford to run out of gas on the highway. Out of state plates, two women and a baby, private detective, the police, the whole country knows who we are."

As the first streaks of dawn flashed in front of them, and the tall buildings seemed so close, yet were still miles away, as the yellow light continued to flash angrily and the gas gauged bottomed below empty, the heavy traffic came to a complete halt as they neared the Lincoln Tunnel.

Al had no choice but to ride along the shoulder, and exit at Weehawken in search of a gas station.

Both the car and Al coasted on fumes as she pulled into a station across the street from a bare bones motel just before the car stalled on its own.

Maddie let out a huge sigh of relief.

Al had already opened the driver's side door to exit, ready to stumble out and pre-pay the gas, when a young man approached.

"What can I get for you?" he asked.

"I don't know you," she said, trying to get her eyes to focus.

"How much gas do you want?"

"You have full serve in New Jersey?"

"Only state I know of," smiled the attendant, who had on a knit Yankee hat and couldn't have been more than eighteen.

"Not true."

"Cash or credit?"

"Cash. Fill it up. No, just twenty dollars. Whatever."

Al shut the door, tilted back on the headrest, closed her eyes.

He opened the gas tank, which was just past the driver's side back window, and inserted the pump.

The next words Al heard were, "Al, Al, we can go now."

She wasn't sure how many times Maddie had been repeating this. With mammoth effort, Al forced her eyes open.

"I have to pay for the gas."

"I already did."

Al appeared dizzy, or at least perplexed. It certainly didn't help that she had started falling into such a heavy deep sleep. She tried to shift the car into *Drive*, then stepped on the gas and was actually steering.

"Al, the car's not on."

She didn't answer, but had trouble locating the keys still in the ignition.

"Al." Maddie leaned forward, was about to touch Al's shoulder but settled for shaking the driver's seat. "I don't think you should drive anymore. We have to go through this long tunnel. Traffic's ridiculous. Who knows how long it will take to find a place to stay?"

"But we're almost safe," said Al. Her eyes fluttered, head bobbed.

"Al!" said Maddie, sharply, causing a snap of her partner's neck. "We have one of two choices. You can let me drive the rest of the way, or we can pull into that motel across the street for some sleep and get a fresh start in a few hours."

"No way," mumbled Al, who began to fumble for the keys one more time in an attempt to start the car.

Maddie waited until Al passed out again. Then went around to the driver's side, coaxed Al out of the car, guided her to the passenger's side, but Al jerked away, used the hood for support, and steered her rubbery legs to the other door, got in.

Maddie slipped into the driver's seat. She forced herself to focus, concentrate on the ritual of starting the car, copying Al from memory.

Foot on the brake. Turn the key. Shift into drive. Accelerate.

There was a little lurch but she made it safely across the street, reversed the car starting process, went into the lobby, checked in, came out with a swipe card for room fifteen. She started the car again and was able to park right in front of room fifteen without a hitch.

She was glad they could rest. She could see the towering New York skyline in the distance, the sun bursting its first rays through the buildings in glorious fashion. They would need all of their energy to handle the bustle of such a big city.

Maddie unlocked the motel door first and left it wide open. She unstrapped a sleeping Jesse, picked him up, then slung his diaper bag and one of their athletic bags over her free shoulder. She also grabbed a plastic bag with sandwiches, more sweets, and juice. Then she persuaded her partner to exit the Honda, Al's eyes blinking rapidly as she staggered into the room in front of Maddie.

Al was so tired she was barely able to form words as she collapsed face first onto the motel bed and muttered, "I'm less unhappy when I sleep."

PART THREE

MOTEL

"Who the hell tipped off the media?" barks Nokenge.

He turns from the motel lobby glass door, clearly disgusted by the reporter frenzy at the gas station across the street, and studies closely the faces of the sheriff, the state trooper, rests a little longer on the deputy, then finally settles on the governor's aide.

"Get your eyes off me," says Peg.

"The motel clerk hasn't moved from the back room," says the state trooper. "I confiscated his cell phone, disconnected the computer."

Nokenge returns to the deputy, who looks extremely uncomfortable.

"I swear I've had no contact with the media," he offers.

"Nothing we can do about it now," says Peg. "except keep them at a proper distance. Let's focus on the task at hand. What do you have on these two so far?"

Nokenge tells the trooper to turn on the lobby TV and monitor the news, then he motions Peg towards a quiet corner of the room.

"I phone interviewed their boss Fox Phelps, who's in deep shit and convinced Al set him up. Says Al's a psycho, Maddie a lost lamb willing to do anything Al says. From what I've seen, and from what happened in Chicago, he's pretty accurate. I spoke to Wynn, the biological father, who seems neutral about Jesse but is certainly enjoying the attention. Says Al can be crazy but has a good heart, and considering what she put herself through to commandeer the sperm, would do anything to keep the baby. The grandfather, Whit, doesn't know shit, but is obsessed with the child and already pursuing legal avenues. Maddie's mother's mentally ill and it's hard to take anything she says seriously after she told me that Maddie was a loyal, doting daughter until she inhaled a bacteria called Al. After seeing a bottle of Seroquel in the motel room, used for bipolar disorder, I tracked down Al's doctor who told me very little because of patient/doctor privilege but believes Al's capable of a wide range of violence."

"Just great."

"See why I've proceeded with caution. She's already threatened the baby in public."

"You do understand," says Peg, "that though it would be unfortunate if the two women didn't make it, it's the baby who's most important. Save the baby, win the day. Lose the baby, we all go down, and this is a re-election year."

"You do understand that I don't give a shit what year it is. My job is to save lives, with Jesse as the priority."

"So what's the plan?"

"I have SWAT personnel in key areas, ready to bust in if we sense the baby's in any danger. The moms are clearly devoted to Jesse, and harming him is doubtful, but I haven't ruled out anything because of Al's unstable nature and Maddie's intense devotion to her partner."

"The longer this is drawn out the bigger this media circus will get."

"And the more likely something crazy can happen. Our best bet is Maddie. I'm working on patching in a phone call to her mother who she's very close with. If I don't feel optimistic, I'll wait for when they've settled, hopefully asleep, and go for the breach with orders to shoot to kill if any move's made to harm the baby."

"Okay," says Peg. "I'll head to the gas station for damage control."

"Sir, I think you should see this," says the trooper.

Nokenge and Peg approach the TV. In the corner of the screen is a superimposed selfie of the deputy with a big grin on his face, the name of the motel barely visible behind him. A reporter says, "This photo was leaked earlier this evening by the wife of the Hudson County Deputy Sheriff who expressed that her husband is a key part of this delicate hostage negotiation."

All eyes rest on the deputy huddled in a corner.

"I told her not to tell anyone. It's my first big case."

Nokenge takes a menacing step in his direction and the deputy starts towards the door. Nokenge turns to the sheriff.

"Take your boy to jail and lock him up. I'll deal with him later."

The sheriff grasps the deputy by the arm.

"Okay, but remember," says the deputy just before being led out, "Weehawken is where Aaron Burr shot Alexander Hamilton."

Al steps away from the motel window.

"How do you think the police knew we were here in the first place?"

"Do you want me to ask Nokenge?" replies Maddie.

"Is he like your best friend now?"

"Al, please."

"Sorry."

The phone rings. Al nods. Maddie picks up.

"I have your mother on the line," says Nokenge. "Would you like to talk to her?"

"Yes, please."

"Hello, Madeline," says a frail voice.

"Are you okay, Mother?"

Al heads to the bathroom to pee, hoping to avoid ripping the phone cord out of the wall.

"They want me to help you."

Mother's words are slurred, which usually happens when her Haldol is increased.

"I'm so sorry you're involved with all of this," says Maddie.

"Are *you* okay?"

"We're all okay. Al, the baby, me."

267

A lump forms in her throat.

"I warned you about the softball coach," admonishes Mother. "Something about her not natural. Something about the baby not natural. Priests and ministers ask me questions. I tell them I'm not lying that you're a virgin, that it's an unnatural conception."

Tears well in Maddie's eyes. Her first reaction is to tell Mother to shut up and that this was why she had to leave Oregon. But she doesn't want to create more stress for someone in her condition.

Al returns, paces, unable to sit.

"I want you to know, Mother, that we're healthy and happy and that I love you very much. Jesse loves you very much as well."

"Who's Jesse?"

"I'll always love you no matter what."

Before Maddie can say goodbye, Mother is gone and Nokenge is whispering.

"Don't hang up. If you think it'll be easier, talk to me like your mother's still on."

"So what have you been doing with yourself lately?" asks Maddie.

"You see the zoo outside. Traffic's at a standstill. The governor's aide is putting on a lot of pressure to resolve this."

"No, I don't know how the police found out we're in New Jersey, Mother. But I wish I knew."

"The gas station attendant across the street called it in to the sheriff's office and then it got to me. He saw the Lancer College parking sticker on the Honda's back window."

"Oh." Maddie looks at Al. "The Lancer parking decal on the car."

Al smacks herself in the head with an open palm.

"Please understand," continues Nokenge, "there's no way Wynn can get full custody. He's a documented drug addict and alcoholic. And grandparents rarely supersede biological mothers. I don't see any way Jesse wouldn't be all yours. As long as you don't do anything *illegal* or *harmful* and we settle this *as soon as possible* in a *peaceful* manner."

"I'm concerned about Al. We're so close. She's done everything to make this dream come true. She loves Jesse with all her heart and Jesse loves her."

"Just tell her to fuck off then hang up," blurts Al.

"Did you know Al procured the sperm without Wynn's knowledge?"

"I assure you I did not."

"All reports indicate you've done nothing illegal. We saw on a security camera who took the plates in the Chicago parking lot. The convenience store clerk told me you tried to stop Al."

"Al's my full partner in this. We're destined to be together. Jesse's as much hers as mine."

Nokenge is at a crossroads. He doesn't want to take a chance on losing what trust he has gained with Maddie, but doesn't want to go overboard with false promises. He believes she can get full custody, but Al is another story. No legal rights, a psychiatric history, stole license plates, knifed someone, threatened the baby publicly, and he would wager she had something to do with Fox Phelps's predicament. Unlikely she would have any part of custody and judging by the tone of the bigoted grandfather, might be excluded from the picture all together.

He needs to lie.

"The New Jersey governor already got the charges dropped in Chicago. The fact that you two live and raise Jesse together makes a strong common law case for both of you to retain custody. The fact that Al's still married to Wynn should make a difference. But you must—let me emphasize *must*—let us in to resolve this situation as soon as possible. I promise to escort all three of you together back to Oregon, keep the media away, and Wynn and Whit out of it as well."

"That sounds wonderful."

"Please understand, Maddie, I'm running out of *peaceful* options."

"I love you!"

Maddie hangs up.

"Can I be spared any more of these conversations?" says Al.

"Sorry."

Jesse gurgles loudly.

"Jesse doesn't want to hear it either."

They laugh.

They walk to him on Al's bed. He stares up and smiles, as beautiful as he has ever been. They smile back. For a moment it feels as if they're in their apartment, alone, bathing in his glow, walled off from the rest of the world, sharing family time, quiet, both sure Jesse will have everything they didn't have, and more.

They hear a huge commotion coming from across the street: boos, cheers, people yelling. Maddie goes to the window. She sees one group marching towards the gas station from the left, another from the right, but can't tell what the uproar is about.

She looks at Al, then looks at the TV.

"I don't give a shit about what's going on out there," says Al.

"It could help to know what's happening."

Al sits on the bed, ogles Jesse.

"Turn it on. But we need to discuss our safety net."

Nokenge watches the marchers through the lobby window. Into a headset he says, "There's a potential riot out there. I'll let you know as soon as there's an opening. All units stay on alert for my signal."

"Copy," says SWAT One from behind the trooper's car in the parking lot.

"Copy," says SWAT Two just to the left of room fifteen.

"Copy," says SWAT Three from behind the tiny bathroom window of room fifteen.

"Roger that," crackles SWAT Four into Nokenge's headset from the roof of the lobby, rifle locked and loaded, finger resting gently on the trigger, barrel pointed straight at the numbers one and five.

Maddie stares at the TV, grateful for the diversion away from a discussion she does not want to have.

On the screen is a group of men and women. There's a close up of a sign that reads *STOP HOMOPHOBIC DISCRIMINATION!*

Then the other group marching is shown. There's another close up of a sign: *LESBOS NO, FATHERS YES!*

The yelling and catcalling from both sides increases in decibels, both groups clearly agitated.

"There's no escaping," whispers Al to Maddie, who sits next to her on Al's bed. "If we give up they'll take Jesse away and who knows who'll get him and when we'll see him again."

"I'm sure we have a good custody case, but we can't exclude Wynn entirely. You said yourself he would never harm Jesse sexually."

Al's head doesn't move, her eyelids peel back, pupils wide open.

"The thought of Wynn being around Jesse makes my bones hurt. He's an addict and a loser who'll never clean up. But I could live with him around once in a while. It's Whit I don't trust."

"We can be there whenever he sees Jesse. He wants an heir. He can provide for his grandson in ways we can't."

"Don't ever call Jesse his *grandson*."

Maddie nods.

Al closes her eyes, fights off something, either another sugar crash, more pain, or more anger.

Maddie wishes desperately that she could hold Al, comfort her, at least reach out with the slightest soothing touch on her partner's hand.

"After my mother died," says Al as she opens her eyes, "and up until the night of my communion, everything I remember about my father was good. He was devoted to me, didn't drink much, took me to the zoo, helped with homework, arranged for a different shift at work so he could pick me up after school. Made me pancakes every Sunday before church."

The thick emotion rising within Al causes her to look away from Maddie and down at the dirty carpet.

"But I came to realize after my communion that from the moment my mother was buried he had a plan. A plan to gain my trust. A plan to make me secure and happy. And that somehow, in his own twisted way of thinking, this would make me agreeable to a childhood dominated by abuse. That somehow he could have a new version of life with my mother. Yeah, I'm sure there was some guilt. Guilt he washed away with his drinking. But that never stopped him from coming to my room. Never stopped him from sparing me just one time no matter how wrecked I was."

Al's voice quivers, but she refuses to cry.

"He would tell me that if I told anyone I would become an abandoned orphan raped by many men and boys. When he suspected that becoming an orphan was preferable to being with him, he promised that he would kill me. And I believed him. Why wouldn't I? He killed me every night he came to my room and

273

fucked me. Sometimes I wished he would've murdered me instead. Sometimes I wished I could've murdered him and me. Then I wouldn't be as vulnerable as I am now."

Still at a whisper, her words grow in power.

"I worked my whole life afterwards not to have dreams or aspirations, hopes that he could destroy, that could lead to more devastation. Then along comes you and Jesse and I care so much about you both, what you think, how you feel, how you feel about me. For the first time I had a clear vision of what was ahead: our perfect life together. And it scared me. Scares me now. Scares me somewhere deep that we might lose it."

Maddie's bottom lip is at full tremble. She wants desperately to find a way to recapture that moment in the Senior Center parking lot when they all embraced, when it was the true birth of their family.

"I understand," says Maddie, "though I know I could never fully comprehend your pain. But don't you see how much better it is to live rather than die?"

Al looks back up from the carpet.

"There's something about Whit that reminds me of my father. Something about Fox as well. All of them want to control everything. All of them pretend to be so righteous. No one, not even my aunt, would ever believe what my father did. And that's what scares me. That even when you think you know someone you still don't, still don't know everything he's capable of."

"I'm never sure what Mother's capable of. And I do understand why as a child you would prefer death over life. But now we have Jesse."

"Why couldn't Whit teach Wynn there's more to life than basketball? Why did he abandon his son so easily when Wynn became incapable of fulfilling his father's dreams? Because he's an egocentric maniac like Fox. Do you want to live with the possibility that Whit hurts Jesse the same way and we allowed it?"

"No."

"Then consider it's better for all of us to be together, always, in a place where no one can hurt us."

"I will. But will you consider that we might get through this together, that Nokenge will do everything he can to help us, and that if we're nice to Whit he might allow us to protect Jesse at all times and live the way we want?"

Before Al can answer, a crescendo of boos rises simultaneously from outside the motel walls and from the TV. Maddie turns towards the TV. Al goes to the window, peeks at the gas station, which has turned into an ocean of media and bystanders. Local police work to maintain order.

"The pandemonium in Weehawken has certainly reached its peak," says the newswoman on TV over the many spectators yelling and waving signs. She is young, dark-haired, completely made up, well dressed, surely out of place in this dingy neighborhood. "To my right are people shouting homophobic slurs and calling for baby Jesse to be taken from what they're calling *the aberrant couple in the motel room* and returned to the true father and grandfather. To my left are gay rights activists and other locals demanding that the *true parents* be allowed to continue their journey and live the life they choose."

She is jostled roughly by the expanding crowd and the microphone is nearly knocked from her hand as thick strands of hair fall over her face.

She stammers, "All of this uproar has escalated with the recent arrival of the unnamed religious group behind me."

The cameraman pans up and there is a crowd of men and women dressed all in white, chanting an indecipherable prayer, carrying cups with lit candles, a poster visible that reads *JESSE BELONGS TO GOD!*

Bumped again, unable to talk clearly over the crowd chaos, the newscaster says, "Charles, I think this is a good time to cut to the interview done earlier today in Chicago."

The TV broadcast returns to the studio and Charles says, "Yes, indeed. Here now is that interview recorded several hours ago by our Chicago affiliate, featuring the alleged biological grandfather who flew directly to Illinois after hearing about the knife slashing incident at a local gas station food mart. Mister—"

"Shit Davis," says Al over the announcer's voice, as she returns to the bed, sits. "Fucking everywhere."

Whit appears on screen in a studio, with Wynn by his side still sporting the same shit-eating grin.

"I'm pursuing every legal avenue to make sure the softball coach can't come within 100 hundred yards of my son, I mean *grandson*. I call on all law enforcement to protect Jesse from this twisted lezzie."

Maddie lets out a slow painful cry. She braces for Al's explosive rant, perhaps a chair through the TV this time.

But Al is unusually quiet, strangely subdued.

She lies flat on the bed, next to Jesse, and closes her eyes, as if begging for more sleep, desperate for anything to rid her of this deep despair.

"Do you understand now why we can't be *caught*? Why we can't be in a world that only wants to control us? Why we can't give up our baby?"

This understanding is as if a giant boulder comes rolling down a hill and flattens Maddie completely.

"Do you understand now how there are only two choices left? We grab Jesse, bolt out this door, run as fast as we can. And just maybe we'll find the freedom we're looking for, somewhere in the dark, or in a hail of bullets that grants us the peace we need."

Maddie crumples to the floor.

"Or we follow through with my plan: clean, sensible, painless, a *safety net* that ensures our family unity forever."

Maddie looks up at her partner, guessing her own expression carries the same weight of Al's, eyes red and moist, the burden of decision adding a sagging elasticity to the weary flesh of their cheeks.

"I know you'll make the right decision," concludes Al.

She closes her eyes one more time.

Maddie can't stop crying.

She does not want it to come to this.

But she has to make a decision soon before Nokenge is forced to do something drastic, or Al takes matters into her own hands.

Maddie picks up Jesse. She holds her warm cheek against his. She looks at the door. Contemplates a third choice: race outside, scream, "Don't shoot!" in the hopes that no one does and they can be safe. But what would Al do? She would never allow herself to be caught. Charge someone and go down in a flurry of bullets? Or maybe use the knife on herself?

It would be cruel and unusual punishment for them both.

"I trust you completely," says Al sleepily. "I trust that you wouldn't run out there without me, that you believe the only answer is all of us together."

This violation would be worse than a hail of bullets for Al.

"I wonder what really would've happened if we made it all the way to New York," adds Al, about to nod off. "Could I manage, or do the scars run too deep? Would there be another Fox or Whit?"

"All three of us together means we can manage anything."

A new roar from outside turns Maddie's attention back to the TV.

Al doesn't budge, knows nothing out there can change what she feels in here.

Whit and Wynn have arrived from Chicago.

Maddie is so stunned she immediately puts Jesse back on Al's bed, afraid she might drop him.

The dark-haired newscaster sidles up to Whit. Father and son beam their smiles and soak up the approval of the men and women who cheer them, ignore those who boo, and remain oblivious to the ones in the white robes who just keep on chanting.

Whit waves a paper in triumph.

"A restraining order! The first giant legal step to make things right!"

Cheers and boos explode.

Nokenge leaves his post at the lobby window, dashes across the street, intent on grabbing both Wynn and Whit and hustling them into the motel lobby office with the state trooper and the desk clerk.

"He'll make sure I never see Jesse again," says Al.

Maddie drags herself to the TV, shuts it off.

"Will you prepare it?" asks Al. "I think it's in my bag."

"I know where it is."

Maddie finds Al's bag, and with trembling hands fishes out two vials of liquid and three syringes.

"There's information with it concerning the dosage for each of us," offers Al, "based on our weight. I did my research. The potassium chloride induces cardiac arrest, while the sodium thiopental is an anesthetic that suppresses the central nervous system and stops

279

respiration so it should be completely painless, and irreversible."

"Can I hold Jesse first?"

"Of course."

Maddie lifts Jesse off of Al's bed again and cradles the infant in her arms, so delicately, so carefully he does not stir one bit from his slumber. But she wants him awake and caresses his cheek with her thumb. He opens his eyes, smiles with so much wonder and joy.

"Hello, precious" says Maddie. "Did you have a nice sleep? We missed you. We love you."

She sits with him on the bed next to Al. She turns his body so he's looking directly at her partner.

"There's Mommy Al," coos Maddie. "You're truly the most blessed child in the universe to have two mommies, two mommies who love you so much. Can you see Mommy Al?"

Jesse laughs and smiles, waves his hand, causes Al to smile back.

"You'll always remember Mommy Al. We've made a promise to be with you forever."

"And I won't break that promise, Jesse."

Maddie sniffs. "He needs a change."

She grabs the diaper bag, takes him into the bathroom for a quick change and diaper disposal.

Al closes her eyes again.

Maddie returns. She bounces with Jesse some more, but he doesn't seem to have much energy. She looks at the three syringes. She looks at the door.

Al can't stop staring at both of them.

"I do understand," says Maddie, "that we're not going to have the life we dreamt about and how difficult that would be."

She places baby Jesse next to Al, who lies down next to him. She brings the vials and syringes to her own bed, begins to prepare them, but has difficulty because her hands shake so much.

Al props herself up on an elbow, stares at her son. His eyes blink and she can't believe he's sleepy again.

"You were so good the whole trip, Jesse. So good to love me the way you do. You never judge me badly. You're always happy around both of us. I'm sorry I never had milk for you in my breasts."

It takes several minutes. Maddie follows the directions carefully, drawing the correct amount of potassium chloride and sodium thiopental into each syringe. She is crying now, again, and her hands are nearly useless, because of Al's intense stare and eagerness, because she really doesn't want to do this.

"Don't cry, my love," says Al. "Imagine the beauty of all three of us together forever."

"Are you really sure?"

"As I've ever been."

"I always believe you know what's best."

When she's done, Maddie shuts the overhead light, leaving on only one lamp by the beds, and brings the prepared syringes over to Al, sits on the edge of her partner's bed.

Nokenge is back at his vigil by the lobby window. He sees the one light go out in room fifteen.

"They're getting ready for bed," says Nokenge into the headset. "Soon, but on my signal only."

He inches out of the office, moves closer to their room. Stops in a dark shadowy area.

"Inject me first," says Al. "If there's discomfort in the end, I'd rather not see it in you and Jesse."

Maddie likes that Al trusts her enough to go first, sure that afterwards she wouldn't just run off with the baby, something that would be devastating to Al in her final moments.

But that doesn't stop her crying, tears torrential as they rain on Jesse's body. She picks up one of the needles, her hand quivering erratically.

"I love you, Al, with all my heart and I always will. Your sacrifices gave us this blessing and I am eternally grateful." Maddie holds the needle out for Al. "But I don't want to be the one to do it to you."

Al takes it, fully composed and without tears.

"I understand. Please don't be sad. We're all going to a place where no one can catch us."

Calmly, Al unbuckles her khakis, pulls them down a bit, along with her underwear.

Maddie inhales a shivery breath; both hands go to her mouth, covering it, stifling a deep, morbid groan.

Al injects the lethal concoction into her left butt cheek.

Maddie's anguish escapes her lips.

"It's okay. It will all be perfect very soon."

Al smiles gently.

"Don't leave me!" cries Maddie.

"I'm not. But you must do it now! So we can be together."

"I want to be together. With you. With Jesse. Forever."

A stiff weakness passes through Al and she knows her strength is ebbing, along with her ability to stop Maddie from leaving, to force Maddie to do it.

"Please. For us. You must! So we can stay together!"

"I'll never leave you."

Before any further hesitation stops her, with Al's eyes riveted on her, Maddie quickly turns Jesse on his side, pulls back his diaper, and with a loud gasp injects him with the second needle, plunging the lever all the way down.

"I love you so much," whispers Al.

Maddie hastily drops her own pants and underwear then injects herself with the last syringe.

"Sealed forever," adds Al. "Thank you for doing this for all of us."

Maddie shuts off the lamp, lies down. All three of them are on the same bed, on their backs, the baby between them. Some illumination streams in from the TV lights across the street.

Nokenge sees the room go dark. Inches closer through the shadows. Whispers into his headset, "Steady. Steady. Just a few moments more so they get settled. Be quick. Be smart. I don't want a mini-Waco."

Jesse is unmoving and barely breathing. Maddie is also perfectly still. Al begins her final stir and Maddie manages to prop up a bit to look at her partner. Al stares back at mother and baby. There's enough light for Maddie to see that there's no distress at all, just a wonderful transformation on Al's face, an appearance Maddie has not seen before.

Al's breathing is even, gradually slowing down, but it's as if all lines on her cheeks, around her eyes, on her forehead have suddenly been smoothed out, replaced by an expression that gives Al a placid beauty.

"It's a new beginning, Jesse," whispers Al. "We're going to a place where we all will be free to be who we want. A place where no one can hurt you, where no one can hurt your mommies."

Al's eyes flutter and they close again. Her speech is stilted, breathing labored, but she is undaunted, truly seeing and feeling everything she says:

"We're going to a place where you can have all the toys you want, all the stuffed animals you need, and magic carpets to take you wherever you want to go. You'll be someone who can dream anything you want, someone who can fulfill all his dreams. I promise you'll always be protected, you'll always be safe. You'll be a child forever."

With preternatural strength, Al lifts herself onto her right side. She looks at Maddie who is barely breathing and whose face is soaked with tears. She looks at Jesse who is perfectly still and content. Using all of her remaining energy—and to the great shock and pleasure of her lover/partner/wife—she leans forward and gives Maddie a tender kiss on the lips. With another surge of exertion, she does the same with precious Jesse. She collapses back onto her shoulder again, but now is able to reach her right hand under Jesse, then under Maddie. She stretches her left arm across the tops of their bodies, grasping Maddie's right shoulder, pulling her to her side, fully embracing them both, arms pulling them so close her hands are able to grasp at the side of Maddie's right arm.

This time it is Al who embraces them into a second but final family hug.

Then she convulses, once, violently, hands breaking their hold, flung onto her back, every muscle seemingly pulled out like a stretched rubber band, her body going taut then suddenly collapsing back in with a snap, shriveling.

Then she is completely still, finally sleeping gracefully with her family. No longer unhappy. No longer part of the world of the living.

All three are lifeless when the motel door is rammed open and two SWAT members pour into the room, guns aimed, lights from their helmets beaming towards the bed in the far corner, Nokenge following from behind.

"Fuck!" shouts Nokenge as he surveys the still bodies and the three used syringes. With desperate urgency he barks into the headset, "Get EMS in here now!"

The monumental weight of her anguish makes it difficult for Maddie to move, but she struggles to prop herself up. She picks up Jesse and he starts to cry.

SWAT One makes a move to grab Jesse from Maddie's arms, but Nokenge—seeing no knife or needle in her hands—tells him to stand down.

Medical personnel rush in and while Maddie stands behind them and convulses into deep sobs, they do their best to revive Al.

But it's too late.

They put her on a gurney and cover her with a blanket.

Nokenge tells everyone to wait outside.

The room is empty, except for Nokenge, Maddie, Jesse, and Al's still body. Nokenge motions for Maddie to sit on the bed closest to the bathroom. Maddie sits. Through her heavy tears she does her best to clutch Jesse to her breast and soothe his crying.

Soon his eyes flutter closed again.

Nokenge sits next to her.

"What happened?"

Maddie keeps her grip rested firmly and confidently around her son.

"Before we left McCannville Al had a suicide concoction delivered that she called a *safety net*, a last resort to keep us together and avoid being part of the world of the *caught*."

"Caught?"

"You'd have to hear her explain it. But I understand her pain. I understand how impossible it would be for her to go on without Jesse and me."

She chokes on her words, hugs Jesse even tighter, gathers herself once more.

"But I knew I could never hurt Jesse and I could never abandon him."

Nokenge places a comforting arm across her shoulder.

"Protesting her safety net back in McCannville would've led to a huge fight and there was no way I was going to stop her from bringing the drugs anyway so I decided to requisition my own FedEx overnight before we left, two movie prop syringes—the kind that make it look like the fluid is injected, but the needle actually retracts—and replace two of Al's needles with fake ones."

Maddie could've gone on to explain how when she changed Jesse's diaper in the bathroom she gave him baby Benadryl to put him out so Al didn't get suspicious, but Nokenge seems to understand everything completely.

"Who injected Al?" he asks.

"She did it herself."

"Stick with that story."

"It's the truth."

"Are you ready to go now?"

"Do I have to talk to reporters?"

"Hell no."

"Where are we going?"

"I have a car waiting to take us to Newark Airport, then I'll escort you and Jesse back to Oregon for a full review of your case. I'll even testify on your behalf if need be."

"Can Al come with us?"

"She expired here so we need to do an autopsy. But rest assured you'll get her back for a proper burial."

Maddie stands, brings Jesse to the side of the gurney. A deep anguished scream within her threatens to explode in a flood of uncontrolled mourning.

"So sad that a chance at life was stolen from her at such a young age."

With a genuine sadness that not all three of them have been saved, Nokenge says, "I'm sorry for your loss."

Maddie pulls the blanket off Al's face. She can't stop staring at her partner. Serene. Content. Beautiful. Smiling.

"It's as if every line and crease of pain has left her."

Maddie leans down and gives Al a long kiss on the lips, a kiss that reinforces the marvelous feeling she experienced moments ago when Al had done the same thing, a sensation Maddie will always carry with her.

"Finally at peace," says Maddie. "An eternal state of grace."

She holds Jesse above Al, face down, so the baby can see his other mother one last time. Jesse touches Al's face and makes the sweetest cooing sound Nokenge and she have ever heard.

"Is it all right if I carry Jesse to the car?"

Nokenge hesitates, knowing he has already broken several rules and that every move once they leave this room will be visually documented.

"Of course."

He also knows that images flashed worldwide of mother holding her son will go a long way in helping Maddie retain full custody.

"Should I take my things?"

Nokenge sees the diaper bag, picks it up, searches through it, sees only diapers and Vaseline and baby powder, and a spare outfit.

"I'll carry this for you. The rest will be returned once our investigation is completed."

Maddie exits first, followed by Nokenge. From across the street there is a blast of sound and light, cameras flashing, people cheering, booing, chanting, making noise. The local police struggle to keep everyone at bay. Peg occupies the media as best as she can by announcing that mother and son are safe, praising Nokenge, mentioning how the governor has made this stand-off his top priority.

Maddie holds Jesse close, his face against her chest, one hand over the other ear, shielding him from the onslaught of sound and light.

With each step across the empty parking lot, towards the white car waiting for them, with hundreds of live eyes on them, and who knows how many through TV, she walks proudly, buoyed with an ever-building pride and strength from being able to protect her son from this assault on the senses.

The white Ford is parked by the motel office.

As they approach the car, Whit, in the lead, followed by Wynn, come storming out of the lobby, the trooper chasing them from behind. Whit waves his piece of paper. Wynn looks at the cameras pointing his way.

"Sir, sir!" shouts Whit at Nokenge. "This document dictates that the softball coach not be allowed in any car, or any plane that includes my grandson!"

All the adults, and the baby, are finally next to each other by the car.

Whit's forceful zeal suddenly vanishes. He drops the hand that holds the restraining order after realizing he is actually in the presence of a tiny, live human being, his flesh and blood that he has obsessed over since first hearing the news.

Everyone becomes fixated on baby Jesse, their attention captured completely by the precious bundle in Maddie's arms.

Perhaps it is the light from all the media equipment pointed their way, the exact direction the lobby entrance spotlight beams down on them, or just the simple glow of this much-loved child that illuminates him above all else around him.

Jesse, like his other mom, is completely at peace, wonderfully content in the embrace of this mother.

Even Wynn, fully enamored, can't take his eyes off the serene beauty of someone so small, perfect, and happy.

Wynn is the first one to turn his head towards the motel room, door open, law enforcement officers moving in and out of number fifteen. The gurney is wheeled out. A forlorn sadness passes across his face. He looks back at Maddie.

She shakes her head.

Nokenge grabs the paper from Whit's hand, tears it up, tosses the shreds at Whit's chest.

"Your restraining order doesn't mean shit in the state of New Jersey. Trooper, escort these two back to the lobby."

The young trooper eagerly follows orders. There is a little resistance by Whit as he glares hard at Nokenge, and the trooper enjoys assisting Whit's retreat with a shove. Wynn follows willingly, his head down.

Nokenge turns towards Maddie, smiles.

"Jesse can't help having a pushy grandfather, but I'd bet my life that once all the details come out you'll be awarded full custody."

Maddie smiles back.

"But before we all *officially* get into the car, I'm afraid I have to take Jesse for now. Lots of people watching."

Maddie takes a long look at Nokenge. Sees the truth and kindness in his eyes.

She takes an even longer look at Jesse's sweet face, fully awake now, pupils wide and full of wonder over what all the fuss is about.

She kisses his forehead, holds him out towards Nokenge, says,

"Please make sure no one hurts the baby."

ACKNOWLEDGEMENTS

I want to thank my dear friend Alan Landes, who while engaged in his ferocious battle with cancer, read the first draft of this novel and took the time to give me wonderful feedback and encouragement. His strength and positivity will always be an inspiration.

I want to thank my father, Sidney Miller, whose ongoing support and belief in me and my writing has made all of the work possible.

ABOUT THE AUTHOR

I.J. MILLER has published five literary works of fiction. SEESAW was translated into German and Spanish and sold over 132,000 copies in the Bantam paperback. WHIPPED is available in English and German. Next came the short story collection SEX AND LOVE, and the novella CLIMBING THE STAIRS. The audio version of WUTHERING NIGHTS was nominated for an Audie Award in 2014. Miller is also a screenwriter, with an MFA from the American Film Institute.

Visit I.J. at ijmiller.com.

Made in the USA
Middletown, DE
27 August 2021